THE PENNY JUMPER

ALSO BY JAMES GRIPPANDO

GONE AGAIN*
CASH LANDING+
CANE AND ABE
BLACK HORIZON*+
BLOOD MONEY*+
NEED YOU NOW+
AFRAID OF THE DARK*+
MONEY TO BURN+
INTENT TO KILL
BORN TO RUN*+
LAST CALL*+
LYING WITH STRANGERS
WHEN DARKNESS FALLS*+
GOT THE LOOK*+
HEAR NO EVIL*
LAST TO DIE*
BEYOND SUSPICION*
A KING'S RANSOM
UNDER COVER OF DARKNESS+
FOUND MONEY
THE ABDUCTION
THE INFORMANT
THE PARDON*

AND FOR YOUNG ADULTS

LEAPHOLES

*A JACK SWYTECK NOVEL
+ALSO FEATURING FBI AGENT ANDIE HENNING

JAMES GRIPPANDO

THE PENNY JUMPER

A NOVELLA

This is a work of fiction. The characters, incidents, and dialogues are products of the author's imagination and are not to be construed as real. Any resemblance to actual persons, living or dead, is entirely coincidental.

 For information address:
Nightstand Press
PO BOX 178122
San Diego, CA 92177

FIRST EDITION

Book design by Gwyn Snider, GKS Creative, Nashville

Library of Congress Cataloging-in-Publication Data
has been applied for.

978-0-9829965-5-3 (hardcover)

978-0-9829965-2-2 (trade paperback)

978-0-9829965-3-9 (mobi)

978-0-9829965-4-6 (epub)

With love,
to the real Ainsley Grace

TABLE OF CONTENTS

THE PENNY JUMPER

A NOVELLA

PROLOGUE

Ainsley Grace wasn't like other four-year-old girls.

Sure, she was adorable in pigtails, loved to color and play games, and she laughed all the way to her toes when you tickled her tummy. But certain differences started to become apparent in preschool. Ainsley had been somewhat of a late talker—late enough for the other mommies to speculate about umpteen disorders that might explain the silence. Then one of the room mothers brought a tray of cupcakes to school for Thanksgiving. The decorative icing on each cupcake was unique: a pilgrim, a turkey, or some other symbol of the holiday. The room mother bent over and presented the tray to Ainsley. "Sweetie, would you like the CHOC—OH—LIT, or the VAH—NIL—LAH?" she asked, thinking that her overworked enunciation might help Ainsley understand.

"I'll have the cornucopia," said Ainsley, as the woman's mouth fell open.

It was as if Ainsley had been observing everything and everybody, studying the entire world around her, and waiting until she had full capability to say exactly what she wanted. From then on, the other mommies, not quite sure what to make of her, referred to her simply as the "most interesting" child they had ever met. It was something Ainsley's mother had known all along.

"Can you read me a story, Mommy?"

Ainsley's mother stopped at the bedroom door, her hand on the knob. They'd already read five books from cover to cover, the lights were out, and she'd thought Ainsley was asleep beneath her pink-and-yellow bunny quilt.

"Please, Mommy. Just one more."

"That's what you said last time, and the time before that."

"I promise. Then I'll go to sleep."

Her mother sighed. Their two-bedroom apartment was a forty-five minute drive from Mt. Evans, and she had to be at the Meyer-Womble Observatory by 5:00 a.m. to finish her research. A doctoral degree in astrophysics didn't come easy. "Okay. One more. A short one."

Ainsley popped up and switched on the lamp. "Earthquakes."

"No. Not again."

"Volcanos."

Her mother smiled. Ainsley had taken an interest in natural disasters, and the book about volcanos had a story of its own—another Ainsley-ism—attached to it. Her very first sleepover had been with her friend Georgia, and Ainsley had selected the bedtime reading. They were about halfway through the part about molten lava pouring into the ocean when Georgia interrupted, as any child might, and asked in frustration, "What kind of a bedtime story is this?"

"How about your book on stars?" her mother asked.

Ainsley's eyes lit up. "Yes! The constellations."

Her mother retrieved the book from the nightstand and climbed into bed beside Ainsley. A stabbing pain in her abdomen made her stop and grimace. This one was bad enough for Ainsley to take notice.

"Are you okay, Mommy?"

Her gynecologist was no alarmist, but he'd nonetheless referred her to a specialist. She'd been forced to cancel the last appointment, and she knew that she needed to follow up. But when was there time? "It's nothing. Just a little tummy wobbles."

She cracked open the book to a full-page photograph of an observatory. Ainsley stopped her before she could turn the page.

"Is that where you're going to work tomorrow?"

"No. But it looks a lot like that."

"Can I go?"

She'd been meaning to take Ainsley at some point, and even though security clearance was fairly tight, she could probably convince the director that a four-year-old was no terrorist threat. "That's a great idea. I'll see if we can go this weekend."

Ainsley cheered. "The telescope there must be ginormous!"

"It is. But it's not the kind you have. You don't put your eye up to it and see Saturn or Mars or the moon. The computers do the looking. And they look way beyond our solar system."

"That's so cool."

"Yeah, it is."

"Mommy, you know what I'm going to do when I grow up?"

"No, but I can't wait to find out."

"Then I'll tell you. I'm going to build the biggest, most amazing telescope in the whole world."

Her mother smiled. "I believe you will, big girl. I truly believe you will."

EIGHTEEN YEARS LATER

ONE

All eyes were on Ainsley Grace, but it didn't make her nervous. She was staring at a desktop terminal, so deep in thought as to be unaware of the half-dozen men watching her, unfazed by the fact that she was the only woman in the room.

"How much longer?" asked Vladimir.

Vladimir Kosov was the founding member of Hilbert Trading Group, a proprietary stock-trading firm that ranked among the most successful of the so-called prop shops. Vlad and his wealthy cofounders hailed from Moscow, and with trading rooms in eleven cities and hundreds more online traders operating from remote locations, Hilbert had a global vision. Ainsley was a consultant to the firm's main office in lower Manhattan, hired to solve the latest challenge in a network of supercomputers that enabled prop shops like Hilbert to compete in an electronic market that was driven by speed.

"Run one more test," said Ainsley.

"Time is money," said Vladimir. "Every time you say 'run another test,' I lose money."

"This is the last one."

Ainsley's task was a puzzler: Whenever a Hilbert trader attempted to purchase a large block of stock at the publicly posted "Ask Price," another buyer would step in instantaneously, buy the stock that Hilbert wanted, and then sell it to Hilbert for a penny more than the original Ask Price. "Penny jumping," as it was called in the industry, wasn't illegal; but, as a computer-programmed strategy, it gave high-frequency trading a black eye. Speed had always been important to traders, but high frequency had ushered in a world in which it still took a lowly human five hundred thousand microseconds to click a mouse; a high-frequency trading algorithm just five microseconds too slow was a dead-bang loser. Some said it was time to replace Wall Street's famous bronze statue of a charging bull with a roadrunner. *Meep, meep!*

"Fine, one more test," said Vladimir. "What are we buying this time?"

"It doesn't matter, as long as it's listed on more than one exchange."

Penny jumping exploited the fact that, unlike the old days of stock tickers and paper trading, a company's stock no longer had to be listed exclusively on the New York Stock Exchange or the NASDAQ. It could be offered on a dozen or more different exchanges simultaneously. The computerized matching system that linked buyers and sellers might fill a buy order for, say, ten thousand shares by pulling thousand-share blocks from a series of exchanges: first, the NYSE; a millisecond later, the BATS; a millisecond after that, the NASDAQ; and so on. Through complex algorithms, the penny jumper "sees" a buy order hit the first exchange, instantly buys up available shares on the other exchanges, and then sells those shares at a lightning-quick profit to the buyer who had placed the order. It was complicated, but Ainsley liked the baseball analogy to explain it to her friends back in Boston.

"Imagine you're outside Fenway," she'd say, "looking to buy four tickets to the Sox game. You don't know it, but some guy follows you and watches you pay a scalper two hundred bucks for two tickets, and he hears you tell the scalper that you need two more. He runs ahead of you to the next scalper, buys up the two tickets you still need, and then quickly sells them to you for one hundred dollars and one cent apiece. You don't really mind the penny-per-ticket surcharge, but if it happens millions and millions of times a day, somebody is getting filthy rich."

Those rich guys are the penny jumpers, high-frequency traders who, in less than a blink of the eye, "front run" orders and shake down other buyers to the tune of billions of dollars, one penny at a time.

Vladimir selected a test stock with the call letters LPM. "Ask price, twenty-six dollars and twenty-nine cents per share," he said, reading from the trading screen in front of them.

"Lift the offer for ten thousand shares," said Ainsley. Her short stint at Hilbert had taught her the trader lingo for "pay the ask price."

Vladimir pressed ENTER. Immediately, an order from another buyer flashed on the screen for ten thousand shares of LPM at $26.30, a penny more than Hilbert's bid.

"Cancel your order," said Ainsley.

Vlad did, and the other buy followed suit. It was happening in milliseconds—thousandths of a second. Clearly the competing buyer was a computer program, not a human being. The dance continued. A new Ask Price popped onto the screen. "Lift the offer," said Ainsley. Vlad did, and so did the other buyer. It was virtually simultaneous, as if Ainsley were giving direction to both traders. But only one order was filled; Hilbert got zero shares. "Cancel it," Ainsley said, and when he did, the Ask Price went back to $26.29.

"Try a hidden order," said Ainsley.

Vlad did, but the penny jumper instantly offered $26.30. This was one virulent HFT program, able to see through an order that was supposed to be hidden from the eyes of other traders. Again Hilbert got nothing. Vlad canceled the order, then did a double take.

"Whoa," he said, his gaze locked on to the screen.

On the screen before them, in plain view, the HFT algorithms were slugging it out. In a matter of seconds, the bid price changed eight hundred times. Each high-frequency trader was trying to position itself at the top of the queue, vying for the one-penny shakedown that the only real buyer in the mix—in this case, Hilbert—would eventually be forced to pay if it wanted to complete its order.

"Enough testing," said Vladimir. "Work your egghead magic."

Magic it wasn't. It was mathematics. Ainsley wasn't a banker or a trader. Until this consulting gig for Hilbert, she'd never even set foot on Wall Street, though it was pretty cool that Vlad's group was named for David Hilbert, whose 1928 "decision problem" shaped the modern algorithm. Ainsley had published a whitepaper about time-synchronization algorithms. Her intended audience had been scientists, particularly those interested in NASA's Kepler Mission and Project Cosmic Company. Kepler was NASA's first mission to find planets in other solar systems that were most similar to planet Earth and most likely to support some form of life. Project Cosmic Company was the land-based complement to the outer-space journey of Kepler, and it involved the coordination of interstellar observations from multiple points around the globe. Ainsley's work had thoroughly impressed her faculty advisor at MIT. Wall Street had been even more impressed. Turns out, time synchronization was not only the key to making sense of interstellar data that moved at the speed of light between multiple observatories, across the continents, and under the oceans. It was also, potentially, the best way to rise above other high-frequency traders.

"Okay," she said. "Try Test Stock Two."

It had taken Ainsley two weeks to create her trading algorithm and write her program. It would take just a millisecond to know whether it worked. Vlad keyed up the order. Test Stock Two was XIG. The Ask Price was $32.92. Hilbert wanted a hundred thousand shares.

"Ready?" asked Vlad.

In the trading-world rainbow, the band of colors was narrow: if you got none of your order, the screen lit up red; part of your order, brown; all of your order, green. Ainsley had come to think of red as the bloody remnants of the HFT shark-feeding frenzy. Brown was the four-letter word that traders used when they got only part of what they wanted. Green was the color of money.

"Lift the offer," she said.

He hit ENTER.

Green. No flurry of penny jumpers. Their order for one hundred thousand shares sailed through at the Ask Price.

"It worked!" shouted Vlad. "This absolutely fucking works!"

The men were jumping up and down, slapping high fives, hooting and hollering. It struck Ainsley as odd, all this celebration over a stock market working the way it was supposed to work, the way the outside world thought that it was actually working. Vlad hugged her tightly and spun her around, a big bear hug from a huge man who easily raised her petite frame from the floor.

"You are brilliant, girl! Fucking brilliant!"

Vlad put her down. She thanked him. The traders raced off to their Bloomberg terminals to make money. Ainsley gathered up her purse and walked to the elevator.

Brilliant. That was exactly what her faculty advisor had told her after he'd read her paper on time synchronization. There had been no bear hug from Professor Bartow, and no roomful of men slapping high fives. Coming from the leader of Project Cosmic Company, the word had meant something to her. She'd felt brilliant.

That morning at Hilbert, she didn't.

Ainsley was eager to pack up her things and head back to Cambridge. The consulting job was over. She'd signed on for this gig believing that she was on the right side of this financial battle. The more she hung around Vlad and Hilbert, however, the more she was coming to think that there was no right side. There were winners and there were losers. Period.

Not that she'd been the first to see the link between telescopes and the trading world. The telescope was a brand-new invention when market merchants started using them to look out to the sea and ascertain the cargo of incoming ships. If the merchant could get a jump on everyone else, determine which goods were soon to arrive on these ships, he could hurry to sell off his supply before the incoming goods flooded the market and drove down prices. Arguably, today's high-frequency traders had nothing on these age-old merchants gazing out to sea.

Did Galileo feel used?

Used. That was probably the word for it. Ainsley wasn't quite sure *how* she was being used, but her gut told her she was—that her algorithm, her creation, would be used in ways she had never intended, and for someone's profit.

What's a girl to do?

Pay off her debt, that's what. Even with scholarships and financial aid, Harvard undergrad followed by MIT had left Ainsley buried beneath a six-figure mountain of debt. A few weeks of consulting work for Hilbert had wiped it away.

The elevator door opened and Ainsley stepped out. Her ride had been without stops, as always. The Hilbert elevator system was state of the art. Passengers punched in a floor number before entering, and an algorithm told them which car to board for an express ride. Algorithms were everywhere. Algorithms ruled.

Ainsley swiped her passkey at the glass entrance doors and entered the main reception area for Hilbert Trading Group. Her temporary office was halfway down the hall, but she couldn't get near it. The hallway was cordoned off and her office doorway was barricaded with taut lengths of yellow police tape. Her office was a crime scene.

"What the heck is going on?" asked Ainsley.

The office manager approached. With him was a handsome African-American man who had the unmistakable, no-nonsense look of an NYPD detective. "That's her," the officer manager said.

The detective flashed his badge and introduced himself as Jenkins. "Ms. Altman, when was the last time you were in your office?"

His tone wasn't threatening, but the question still felt like an accusation to Ainsley. "Last night. Why?"

"Your computer is gone," said Jenkins.

"What?"

Ainsley rose up on her tiptoes and peered over the detective's shoulder, grabbing a glimpse into her office. The box that usually sat on her desktop was gone. Wires were dangling over the edge.

"It was there last night," she said.

"So you admit you were here after hours," the officer manger said.

"Yes. I was working. I know the rules. None of my work can go home with me on a laptop. Everything has to be done right here in the office."

"On the Hilbert computer," said Jenkins.

"Right."

"Which is now missing."

"Apparently," said Ainsley. "I have no idea what happened to it."

Jenkins and the office manager exchanged glances. Ainsley

was starting to feel like a suspect. Brilliant wasn't even a distant second.

Jenkins put away his notepad. "Ms. Altman, I'd like you to come down to the station with me."

"Why?"

"I think it's important."

"Why?"

The office manager took a half step forward, interjecting. "Are you hiding something, Ainsley?"

"No!"

"Then why won't you cooperate?"

"I didn't say I wouldn't."

Jenkins tried a softer approach. "It won't take long, Ms. Altman. Will you come with me, please?"

A crowd of workers had gathered at the end of the hall, watching. The office buzz was about to launch. Going downtown with Detective Jenkins seemed preferable to hanging herself out on the grapevine in plain view.

"Okay," said Ainsley. "Let's go."

TWO

Ainsley climbed out of the backseat of Detective Jenkins's car and immediately smelled spring rolls. The NYPD Fifth Precinct was in Chinatown, and Ainsley was *that* hungry. Forgetting to eat was normal when Ainsley was nearing the completion of a project, and she'd held true to form on the penny jumper program. As she followed the detective up the stairs and into the precinct house, however, it suddenly occurred to her that her next meal might be a bologna sandwich on soggy white bread in the Manhattan Detention Complex. She shook off the thought.

You've done nothing wrong.

The Fifth Precinct was Manhattan's oldest, operational since 1881, and the lobby was straight out of cop-show classics: uniformed police officers coming and going, two prostitutes in a territorial dispute, a drunk with a bloody nose, and a homeless guy with vomit all over his shoes sitting on the end of a long wooden bench. Jenkins escorted her past the daily circus and led her down the hall to an interrogation room. As soon as they entered—not an HFT millisecond later—Ainsley realized that Jenkins had lied to her: this trip downtown would *not* be quick. The FBI was involved.

It was just the three of them in the small, brightly lit room: Ainsley sat on one side of the rectangular table; Detective Jenkins and FBI Special Agent Michael Salazar were seated on the other. Ainsley could only assume that any number of law enforcement officers were watching and listening from behind the one-way mirror that faced the doorway. Special Agent Salazar started things off with an introduction, the intent of which seemed to intimidate her.

"I've been with the FBI for more than a decade," he said, "most of it with the securities fraud squad. For your own good, I want you to know up front that I'm highly trained in the means and methods by which individuals use computers and the internet to commit federal offenses, including the theft of trade secrets and the interstate transfer of stolen property. Are we clear?"

"I guess so."

"Good."

The next forty minutes was an exercise in tag-team interrogation. Ainsley answered all of Salazar's questions, then Jenkins' follow-up questions, and then Salazar's follow-ups to the follow-ups. She assumed that the redundancies and constant revisiting of certain points of inquiry were not without purpose; clearly they were trying to catch her in an inconsistency. Unable to trip her up, Salazar left the room, seemingly annoyed. Jenkins said nothing during the agent's absence. He seemed content to let the subject stew in silence. Ainsley hoped it would be the end of the matter. Finally, Salazar returned with an iPad, which he laid on the table in front of her.

"I have additional questions for you," he said. "But first, let me show you this."

"What is it?"

"Video from Hilbert Trading's security cameras."

Ainsley watched as Salazar pulled up the video on the screen and hit PLAY. There was no audio, and the black-and-white image had the grainy quality that was typical of security cameras, but it was clear enough. The initial frames showed a man dressed in a heavy black winter coat, his head covered by a knit cap. He was standing outside the locked entrance doors to Hilbert Trading Group. The date stamp in the lower right-hand corner of the frame said 3:47 a.m.

"Any idea who that is?" asked Salazar.

The hat made it difficult to see the man's face. "None," said Ainsley.

The video continued to play. The man slid a passkey through the electronic reader and opened the door. Salazar froze the frame. "Do you have a Hilbert passkey, Ms. Altman?"

"Yes. So does everyone who works there."

"Did you ever lend yours to anyone?"

"No, absolutely not."

He hit PLAY again. The image skipped ahead. The next frames were from a different camera: 3:49 a.m. The man was still wearing his winter coat and hat, but he was standing in the hallway outside the door to Ainsley's office. He slid the passkey through the reader. Then he opened the door and entered. Salazar hit PAUSE.

"Are you sure you never loaned your passkey to anyone?"

"Never."

"Hilbert tells us that each employee's security card is programmed to open the main doors and the door to the employee's assigned office. Is that your understanding?"

"Yes."

"So if you never loaned your card to anyone, how do you explain this fellow having a passkey to your office?"

"I lost my card about ten days ago."

"Did you report it stolen?"

"Yes. Hilbert canceled the old card and issued me a new one. That's obviously what happened here. Somebody found my lost card and figured out a way to reactivate it. Then they used it to enter my office and steal my computer."

Salazar smiled a little and shook his head.

"Why is that funny?" asked Ainsley.

His expression turned more serious. "Ms. Altman, somebody broke into Hilbert Trading Group just before four o'clock this morning, and they took exactly *one thing*: your computer. Do you understand that?"

"I do now."

"So what you're saying is that some bad guy decided to steal your computer. By absolute luck, he happened to find a Hilbert passkey and was able to get inside the building. And then, in an even more incredible stroke of luck, the passkey turned out to be the key to *your office.* Is that your story?"

Ainsley hesitated. Even she didn't believe it, but then it dawned on her. "My passkey must not have been lost."

"You just told us it was lost and you reported it as lost to Hilbert."

"I thought it was lost. It must have been stolen. Somebody stole my passkey with the intent to reactivate it and come back to steal my computer."

"Who?"

"I don't know who. That's *your* job. Obviously, it was somebody who wanted the information on my hard drive."

"Exactly what was on your hard drive, Ms. Altman?"

"Everything I've done for Hilbert since I signed on as their consultant. We agreed to a very strict confidentiality protocol. All my work would be done in their office and on their computer."

"To be clear," said Salazar. "Whoever has your computer has the program you wrote for Hilbert."

Ainsley swallowed hard. Hearing it from an FBI agent made it sound about as bad as it could sound. "I'm afraid that's true."

"I see," said Salazar. He retrieved the iPad and put it aside. "Do you know how much money penny jumpers make?"

"A penny?"

"Cute," he said. "The FBI estimates that those pennies add up to about one hundred sixty million—*every trading day.*"

It was a guesstimate Ainsley had heard before. "That's a lot of money."

"Yes, it is. So let me tell you what I think happened. Hilbert paid you a hundred thousand dollars to write a program that beats the penny jumpers. You realized that job one of the penny jumpers would be to beat your program, which would be easy if they had your code in their own hands. And you also realized that they would pay you a lot more than a hundred thousand dollars to get it."

"That is completely untrue."

"You're well aware of what happens to employees and consultants who walk out the door with source code on their laptops. I, personally, arrested an HFT programmer at Goldberg Stack for doing exactly that. So you hooked up with someone on the outside and staged this break-in."

"I would never do anything like that."

"Who's your buddy, Ms. Altman? Give me a name, or this is going to get really messy for you."

"Are you saying I'm under arrest?"

"Let's walk through some specifics," said Salazar. "Starting with . . ."

Ainsley's head was spinning. The motive sounded plausible, and even though Salazar had ignored her question about an arrest, he clearly had an agenda. Part of her wanted to go toe-to-toe with him and not only deny, but disprove, everything. While at Harvard, however, she'd dated a law student who'd since gone on to become quite a sharp criminal defense lawyer in New York. One night, after watching the nonstop media coverage of the Amanda Knox murder trial in Italy, they'd had a spirited discussion about innocent people getting arrested. Connor had clearly thought it was more common than Ainsley did, but she remembered what he'd told her to do if *ever* she was taken into police custody for *anything*, not matter how small.

"Excuse me, Agent Salazar," said Ainsley.

He stopped talking.

Ainsley knew what the FBI would think—that she had

something to hide—but this wasn't the time to dig herself out of the hole that she'd been pushed into.

"I want to talk to an attorney," she said.

THREE

The first thing Ainsley did was get out of that police station. Then she called the Law Office of Connor Jameson, P.A. Actually, she followed her nose into Chinatown to find those spring rolls that had beckoned, and then she called Connor. They met at Fing Joo Restaurant and took a table by the window, neither one noting the perfect and somewhat ironic view of the squad cars that were parked right outside the Fifth Precinct, directly across the street.

"Thanks for coming over so fast," said Ainsley.

It had started to snow outside—the third storm since the official beginning of the spring that refused to be sprung—and Connor brushed a few wet flakes from his thick brown hair. "No problem. Happy to help an old friend."

Old friend. Technically speaking, she was no more than that, but it sounded strange coming from someone who might well have made it to the top of her "rest of my life" list. Connor had graduated from Harvard Law on the same day Ainsley had received her undergraduate degree. She'd asked him to stay in Boston so that she could do postgraduate work at MIT. He'd asked her to come to New York so that he could take a job with the U.S. Attorney's office in Brooklyn. Two really smart people could surely lick this problem, but three-hour train rides between Boston and Penn Station clearly weren't the solution.

Connor needed to be back at the courthouse by 1:00 p.m.—he'd recently left the U.S. Attorney's office to do criminal defense—so there was no time for small talk. The smell of spring rolls that had lured Ainsley across the street was actually dim sum, Fing Joo's specialty. Their Cantonese server brought them bubble tea, and Ainsley gave Connor the broad background while they waited for their food.

"The FBI has been all over these types of cases lately," said Connor. "It started when they indicted some HFT programmer at Goldberg for loading source code onto his computer and taking it to his new job at another HFT firm."

"Agent Salazar mentioned that one."

"The case went to trial when I was still at the U.S. Attorney's office. The good news for you is that his conviction was eventually reversed on appeal. The bad news is that the ordeal pretty much ruined his life. Got divorced, filed for bankruptcy, no one would hire him."

"Thanks. With that kind of bedside manner, you should have been a doctor, not a lawyer."

He smiled. "Hey, I thought big girls don't whine."

It was one of Ainsley's rules to live by, much more than a mere expression. She'd been saying it since she was a child, since that night she'd climbed up into the hospital bed to be with her mother one more time, and her mother had told her that tears were OK, that big girls *do* cry. They just don't whine.

"I'm not whining," she said. "Just making an observation."

The server brought their food and left quickly, without a word—no "*Can I bring you anything else?*" or even the obligatory "*Enjoy your food.*" She was clearly in her busy-lunchtime zone.

"Do you want me to contact the FBI as your lawyer?" asked Connor.

"Would you do that for me?"

"Of course."

"Is that what you recommend? We reach out to them?"

"Absolutely. You and I need to talk more about this after I get out of court this afternoon. But based on what you've told me, it's obvious that this problem isn't going to just go away by itself."

"Unfortunately, I have to agree. But wait: How much do you charge?"

"It varies. I do require a retainer, which in this case I would set at . . . having dinner with me tonight."

"Isn't there some kind of ethical rule against that?"

"Only if we have sex. But you'd be worth a lost license."

"Oooh-kay."

Connor splashed soy sauce on his dim sum. Ainsley was reaching for her chopsticks when she noticed Agent Salazar enter the restaurant.

"Don't look now . . ."

"What?" asked Connor.

Salazar brushed the newly fallen snowflakes from his coat and walked straight toward their table. Two men in uniform were right behind him. Ainsley's heart raced as they stopped and stood beside her. Then Salazar spoke.

"Ainsley Altman, you have the right to remain silent. Anything you say can and will be used against you in a court of law."

"Excuse me?"

Customers at nearby tables stopped talking and looked.

"You have the right to an attorney," said Salazar.

"I'm her attorney," said Connor, "and this grandstand play is totally unnecessary."

More customers were watching as Salazar continued. "If you cannot afford an attorney . . ."

The agent kept talking, but Ainsley was almost deaf to him, numb to the harsh reality of what was happening to her. "Connor, what do I do?"

He reached across the table and took her hand, forcing her to look him straight in the eyes. "Stand up and go with him, and the only thing you are to tell anyone is that you are speaking *only* through your attorney."

She rose. The federal marshal cuffed her hands behind her back. The entire restaurant was watching. Connor glared at Salazar with red-faced anger, but he kept his voice down so as not to create a scene.

"This is bullshit. Arresting her in a public restaurant? Really? She would have surrendered voluntarily. You're treating her like a fugitive about to flee the country."

"She brought this on herself," said Salazar. "She's booked on the eleven p.m. flight from JFK to Taipei."

"What? No, I'm not," said Ainsley

"Yes, you are, and for obvious reasons. Taiwan is one of the few countries that doesn't require a visa and, more to the point, doesn't have an extradition treaty with the U.S.."

"I didn't buy a ticket to Taiwan. The only place I'm going is back to Cambridge. Connor, this is—"

Connor flashed the "cut" sign, stopping her in midsentence.

"Please come with me," said Salazar.

Ainsley wanted to speak, but she followed Connor's advice and started walking. Customers raised their cell phones and iPads to snap photographs and record video of the social-media high point of their day. Ainsley was suddenly no different from any of those criminals she'd seen on the nightly news, head down and walking in shame in the company of law enforcement.

"I'm right behind you," said Connor.

Ainsley was shaking on her way to the exit, and as the makeshift paparazzi recorded her every movement on the way to jail, her only solace was that, no matter how many posts and hits she drew on the internet, her mother would never see them.

I'm glad you're here, Connor.

FOUR

Hong Kong. It was Vladimir Kosov's favorite city—for the time being, anyway. His favorite spot in the world changed with the market, wherever he and Hilbert could make its next billion.

"Tseung Kwan O Industrial Estate," he told the driver.

He settled into the seat as the black limousine pulled away from the curb. Even though he'd slept through most of the sixteen-hour flight, he was still a little jet lagged, having left JFK at 3:00 p.m. and landed at Hong Kong International at 7:00 p.m. But he was rested enough to do business. Big business.

The driver followed the northern route from the airport. It was nearly an hour's drive to the industrial estate, but the view of Hong Kong Island to the south, from across Victoria Harbor, was breathtaking. Nestled on the waterfront, at the foot of a mountainous peninsula, Hong Kong boasted more skyscrapers than any city on earth. It was the end of another business day in the financial district, but the skyline was coming to life in the afterglow of an orange sunset, hundreds of glass towers glistening from top to bottom with countless squares of light. The lights faded as they continued around Junk Bay to the industrial estate.

Junk Bay. The name made Vladimir chuckle. It reminded him of Michael Milken and junk bonds, Wall Street thievery 1980s style. Those guys were punks compared to Hilbert.

The limo stopped in front of a dark warehouse. Tseung Kwan O Industrial Estate wasn't "industrial" in the nineteenth-century/Andrew Carnegie sense of the word. It was a mix of low-rise office buildings and warehouses, home to local television stations, an assortment of media companies, banks, and other businesses, none of which seemed to mind the fact that they were sitting on landfill. It was also the site of a three-story, state-of-the-art data center that served the Hong Kong Stock Exchange. If all went according to Vladimir's plan, Hilbert Trading Group would soon be the data center's next-door neighbor.

"Keep the change," he told the driver. Cash. It was how he always paid while on business: no credit-card trail.

The driver thanked him, got back in his limo, and drove away. Vlad checked his Rolex, straightened his tie, made sure that no more than a quarter inch of linen showed from the sleeves of his hand-tailored silk suit, and walked toward the entrance with his chest out. Through a prior exchange of e-mails he'd arranged a meeting with the owner of the property, Mr. Chen, who was standing on the front step, waiting with a smile.

"Good evening and welcome, Mr. Smith," Chen said in rapid-fire English with a Chinese accent.

Yes. Vladimir Kosov from Moscow was Tom Smith from New Jersey. Creative aliases were not his strong suit.

"Please, Mr. Smith. You come inside."

"No need," said Vlad.

His finger froze on the security keypad. "No come inside?"

"I'm here to close a deal. Not to take a tour."

"You want to buy now?"

"Right now," said Vladimir.

"Okay. You pay fifty million dollar, we close deal."

Vladimir buried his hands into his pants pockets, as if he might just have that much cash on him. Then his gaze drifted toward Junk Bay. "Actually, I would like to see the waterfront."

"Yes, yes, I show. This property only one for sale with heliport and waterfront."

Vladimir nodded and then followed Mr. Chen around the building. He hadn't known about the heliport. Not that it mattered.

A cool breeze wafted in from the bay as they rounded the building and headed toward the seawall at the northern lot line. Twilight had completely given way to darkness. In the distance, a scattering of colored running lights from otherwise invisible vessels dotted the black waters of Junk Bay. Much closer were the security lights of the data center next door.

"This is exactly the location I'm looking for," said Vladimir.

They stopped at the waterfront and gazed out toward the bay.

"You mean co-location," said Chen, smiling thinly.

Colocation. It was a term that would have meant nothing to Vladimir just five years earlier. Almost overnight, it had become an obsession. HFT firms were investing millions of dollars in the fiber-optic cable that transmitted their orders to the exchanges at the speed of light. It didn't take an overeducated quant to figure out that shortening the distance between Point A and Point B would reduce the travel time of data. Colocation, or colo, was industry lingo for getting as physically close as possible to the data centers and, ultimately, to the computer exchanges where electronic trades were made. Optimal colocation might shave off only a fraction of a millisecond, but among high-frequency traders, there was no prize for second place: a nanosecond lag time might as well be a year and a day.

Chen's reference to colocation signaled that he knew exactly what his land was worth.

"My offer is twenty-five million," said Vladimir.

Chen smiled again. "You high-frequency guys kill me. Always try to shave off pennies. My price, fifty million."

"The going rate for waterfront here is less than four hundred dollars a square meter."

"Five other HFT guys visit here last week, want to buy. My price firm."

"No negotiation?"

"No, Mr. Smith. No negotiation."

"Hmm." His gaze turned once again toward the black bay. A sudden burst of breeze lifted Vladimir's necktie, and then the night went still. A man dressed in black emerged from the darkness. Chen watched with an uneasy eye as the silhouette approached. Vladimir remained a picture of cool. His man was on time.

"Who coming there?" asked Chen.

"Be nice," said Vladimir. "The poor guy just finished a

two-hour meeting with his parole officer. He can't be in a good mood."

The man walked toward Chen and stopped just a few feet away. Muscles bulged from beneath his tight black sweater. Leather gloves covered two enormous fists. Chen was of small stature, but the man made even Vladimir look slight.

Chen glanced nervously at Vladimir. "Who is this man?"

"Mr. Chen," said Vladimir. "Meet my negotiator."

FIVE

Ainsley lost track of time.

The FBI had taken her straight to the federal detention facility in lower Manhattan, and from the moment she'd entered the multi-story building, she'd felt untethered from reality. No watch. No cell phone. No talking allowed. She especially didn't like the way the correctional officer was looking at her. It wasn't the first time a man had undressed her with his eyes, but in this situation, where she was literally his prisoner, it was especially creepy.

Why do they need male guards for female inmates?

The hours passed slowly, even though they'd kept her moving. Up and down several flights of stairs. In and out of different holding pens. She'd been shackled, unshackled, and shackled again. The body search had been especially memorable, not so much for what actually had happened, but for fear of what might. Fingerprinting took another hour. The state-of-the-art machine kept delivering error messages: rolling too fast, too slow, not a clear image, multiple fingers detected (odd, since her other fingers weren't even on the screen), partial finger detected. Finally, she was allowed to make a phone call. She rang her faculty advisor at MIT. She wondered what Professor Bartow must have thought when his caller ID flashed "Metropolitan Correction Center" and he heard his protégé's voice on the line.

"Professor? It's me."

"Ainsley?"

Oh, God. She didn't know how she could possibly tell him the news, but as it turned out, she didn't have to say much of anything. Professor Bartow already knew.

"I've seen the press release. The FBI's public information office e-mailed it to me twenty minutes ago."

"They issued a *press release*?"

"Yes. It's actually a joint release from both the FBI and the U.S. Attorney's office."

"I must be the talk of the campus."

"I'm afraid it's a bit wider than that."

Of course it was. *MIT Physicist Arrested for Stealing Secret Wall Street Code.* A headline that catchy would surely go viral. "I can't believe this is happening to me."

"Don't worry about things you can't control. Do you have a lawyer?"

"Yes. A friend who lives here in New York. Connor Jameson."

"Is he any good?"

"Very good."

"Okay. I'll see if I can get the department to cover the expense."

A lump came to her throat. He was effectively saying "*I believe in you; I know you're innocent.*"

"Thank you."

"You don't have to thank me. When is your bail hearing?"

"Connor says it will probably be first thing tomorrow morning."

"So you're spending the night in . . ."

He didn't want to say it any more than she did, but one of them had to. "Yes," said Ainsley. "In jail."

"Okay. We'll get through this," he said. "Where's the courthouse?"

"Downtown. Foley Square. It's literally across the street from the detention center."

"Okay. I'll take the train down. I'll be there tomorrow morning."

"That would mean a lot. Thank you."

They said good-bye. Ainsley hung up and waited by the phone for the corrections officer to come. And waited. And waited some more. Connor had warned her about the overcrowded conditions at MCC, and Ainsley guessed they were having trouble finding a bunk for her. It was "lights out" by the time the guard finally arrived and took her to her cell. The cell door buzzed open. Ainsley entered quietly, trying not to disturb the inmate on the top bunk as she climbed onto the mattress below. It squeaked as she settled in. The cell door closed, and then it hit her. She was locked behind bars with . . .

Bonnie Parker? Lizzie Borden? Lindsay Lohan?

She didn't want to know. Try as she might to fill her mind with happy thoughts, she could think only about the press release Professor Bartow had mentioned—and even worse, about the way it was surely being embellished as news worked its way from New York and Boston all the way back to her hometown in Colorado. Her entire life, Ainsley had always been the little girl who'd been dealt a rotten hand in life and nonetheless made something of herself. Duke Tip Kid. Perfect score on the SAT. Valedictorian of her high school class at the age of sixteen. A star at Harvard and handpicked by the renowned Professor Bartow for postgraduate studies at MIT. The refrain among friends and strangers alike had always centered on the same heartwarming sentiment: Her mother would have been so proud.

And now, this.

Even if the truth finally won out and she was eventually vindicated, would anyone ever remember that her name had been cleared? Of course not. They would remember only the MIT astrophysicist who was charged with stealing trade secrets on Wall Street. Forevermore, she would be Ainsley Grace, "Code Thief."

She tried to close her eyes, but each time she did, even for a minute, her overactive imagination unleashed a slew of prison nightmares. Connor had told her what to expect, but not even the most seasoned criminal defense lawyer could have prepared her fully for that first night behind bars. Connor didn't know jail firsthand, and he couldn't possibly grasp the things that were being seared into Ainsley's memory with the passage of each agonizing minute. The odor from her pillow, which had somehow absorbed the stench of the prison toilet. The lonely echo of footfalls as the guards made their rounds. The scary voice of the woman in the top bunk.

"What'd you do, pretty girl?"

It startled Ainsley. Presumably, the woman wanted to know

what crime she had committed, and Ainsley didn't want to go there. The even bigger fear was that her voice might crack and that she would sound weak in a place where only the strong survived. She answered with a question that would make her sound tough.

"I'm no pretty girl. Why are you calling me that?"

"Yeah, you is. I saw you walk in. Fuckin' pretty girl."

The woman had only pretended to be asleep. Ainsley kept quiet, hoping her cellmate would let it drop. No such luck.

"So, what'd you do to land yourself in here?"

"Nothing," said Ainsley.

The woman chuckled. "Just like the rest of us." She hung her head over the edge of the mattress and peered down at Ainsley, her long dreadlocks dangling in the shadows. "Come on, pretty girl. You can tell me."

"Really, I didn't do anything."

"Cocaine?"

"No."

"Prostitution across state lines?"

"No!"

The woman's smile drained away. "You think I'm a snitch, don't you?"

"What? No, I—"

"Fucking bitch. You go around callin' people a snitch, you better watch your skinny backside."

Ainsley lay awake in the prison silence. It was dark. It was scary. Her pillow stunk so badly that she had to throw it on the floor. Maybe her cellmate had sprinkled it with toilet juice: the joke's on the newbie, the pretty girl.

Watch your backside.

The shame of it all was bad enough. Fear was an unwelcome addition to the mix. But it kept circling back to shame. All her life, Ainsley had been a problem solver. This was a problem she didn't understand. It was beyond frustrating. It bordered on terrifying, and she couldn't stem the emotions that were welling up inside and begging to escape. The very words that she and Connor had joked about in his office just a few hours earlier were echoing inside her head. Mom was right. Fergie and her hit song were so wrong.

Big girls do cry.

Ainsley struggled to hold it in, but a tear fell in the darkness. And then another.

SIX

On Tuesday morning Ainsley was brought from her cell to the basement of the Metropolitan Correction Center. Her bail hearing was set for 9:00 a.m. before U.S. Magistrate Judge Shelly Larkin.

A tunnel forty feet below ground connected the jail to the Thurgood Marshall United States Courthouse. Shackled at the ankles, cuffed at the wrists, and chained at the waist, Ainsley shuffled down the long corridor in silence, flanked by marshals. They stopped in front of a surveillance camera, and a guard buzzed them through an electronic door that led to an elevator. The metal doors cranked open, Ainsley stepped into the cage, and the doors closed with an even greater racket. The electric motor hummed and her mind raced as they ascended into the courthouse. The elevator stopped, and as the doors parted, Ainsley was relieved to see Connor standing on the other side. She walked straight toward him.

"I have to get out of this place," she said in low but firm voice.

"I have a plan. Trust me on this."

A marshal led the way into the courtroom. It was an impressive old room with high ceilings and a long mahogany rail that separated the public seating from the business end of the justice system. The judge had yet to arrive, but the prosecutor was seated at the government's table in front of the empty jury box. FBI agent Salazar was with him. Ainsley followed her lawyer through the swinging gate, went to the opposite side of the courtroom, and took a seat beside Connor at the defense table. The guards left them alone.

"Who's the prosecutor?" asked Ainsley, her voice just above a whisper.

"Ben Goodkin," said Connor. "He heads the complex fraud unit at the U.S. Attorney's office."

Ainsley sized him up quickly: mid-forties with no wedding ring, and the vaguely athletic build of a former jock who could no longer find time to exercise, all of which added up to a career prosecutor who was married to his job. "He must be good."

Connor didn't answer.

A scattering of spectators watched from the gallery. Cameras were not allowed in federal court, but the press section was full. Not all were staring at Ainsley, but it felt as if they were. She tried not to make eye contact with anyone, but Professor Bartow caught her attention from his bench seat in the back row. He'd kept his promise to be there for her. The professor had a special connection to Ainsley. He and Ainsley's mother had collaborated on their research at the Meyer-Womble Observatory in Mt. Evans, Colorado, while they were doctoral candidates at MIT. He'd credited her posthumously with lead authorship on their whitepaper that was published after ovarian cancer had taken her life.

Connor leaned closer, speaking softly. "See those guys over there?"

He was indicating a handful of men in the first row of public seating, just on the other side of the rail behind the prosecutor's table.

"Who are they?"

"Lawyers for Hilbert Trading Group. Latham, Moore, and Sterling. Big Wall Street firm. Looks like the U.S. Attorney's office has brought in reinforcements."

Ainsley was starting to feel outgunned.

A crisp knock echoed from behind the judge's bench. The paneled door to her chambers swung open, and the bailiff called the proceeding to order.

"All rise!"

The courtroom fell silent, everyone standing as Judge Larkin ascended to the bench. The clerk called the case, and the sound of it—"United States of America versus Ainsley Grace Altman"—gave her chills. Judge Larkin offered a clipped "Good morning," counsel announced their appearances for the record, and they moved straight to business.

"May I have the date and time of Ms. Altman's arrest?" the judge asked.

"Yesterday at approximately twelve-ten p.m.," said the prosecutor.

"Ms. Altman, the purpose of the proceeding is to advise you of certain rights that you have, to inform you of the charge made against you under the Economic Espionage Act, and to determine under what conditions, if any, you might be released before trial. Do you understand?"

Espionage? It made her sound like a spy.

"Does the defendant understand?"

"Yes, Your Honor," said Ainsley.

"You have the right to remain silent," the judge said, and for the second time in as many days, Ainsley stood and listened to the full recital of her Miranda rights. Again the judge asked if she understood, and Ainsley did, but anyone who thought that Ainsley would stand around and remain silent certainly didn't understand Ainsley.

"I'd actually like to say something," she whispered to her lawyer.

"Don't."

The judge glanced toward the prosecutor. "Mr. Goodkin, what is the government's position on bail?"

"We seek detention, Your Honor. Ms. Altman is both a danger to the community and a flight risk."

"How is she a danger to the community?"

"Because of the way this stolen program interfaces with the various markets and exchanges, it could be used to manipulate markets in unfair ways. Right now that code is in the hands of Ms. Atlman's alleged accomplice, who may or may not know how to use it. If the defendant is released, there is a clear and convincing danger that she will meet up with her accomplice and facilitate the sale of the stolen code to a third party who will misuse it in ways that are detrimental not only to Hilbert but also to the financial markets as a whole."

The judge didn't seem impressed. "Clear and convincing, huh? Not to me. Unless you have a much stronger argument on flight risk, this is going to be a short hearing."

"The defendant most definitely is a flight risk. At the time of her arrest, she had already booked a flight to Taiwan, a country that has no extradition treaty with the United States. She has no family ties here. Her mother died when she was a child, and she was raised by her maternal grandmother, who is now deceased. Her parents never married, and she has had only incidental contact with her father. She is not married and has no children. As I mentioned, she stands to derive substantial profit from selling the code to any number of third parties who may misuse it. She is facing serious jail time if convicted, and there is substantial evidence that she is guilty of the charges she faces."

The judge jotted down a few notes and then looked at Connor. "What about that flight to Taiwan, Mr. Jameson?"

"We dispute that my client actually booked that flight," said Connor.

"So Mr. Goodkin is lying? There was no ticket purchased?"

"No, Your Honor. The ticket was purchased, but we deny that Ms. Altman purchased it. Somebody purchased it in her name to make it look as though she is guilty of something. This is a setup."

"I see."

It was the judicial "I see," which basically translated to *"I've seen it all, and I've definitely heard that one before."*

Connor continued. "Furthermore, my client has no prior arrests and no prior connection to the criminal justice system. This is a trade-secret case, not a murder case. We will be happy to surrender Ms. Altman's passport to the court pending trial."

"Can I say something?" asked Ainsley.

"No," Connor whispered.

"But I want to," she whispered back.

The judge seemed to intuit the substance of their exchange, and, for whatever reason, perhaps to protect Ainsley from herself, the judge sided with Connor. "Ms. Altman, this is just a bail hearing. You'll have the opportunity to address the court and the jury, if you wish, at a future time."

Ainsley paused. *You have the right to remain silent.* She was no lawyer, but she'd seen the cast of characters on TV news who had walked that same tunnel she'd just walked from the detention center, stood in this same courtroom, and invoked that right to say nothing. Gambino family crime boss John Gotti. Ponzi scheme mastermind Bernard Madoff. The list went on. She wasn't going to be on it.

"With all due respect, Your Honor, the purpose of this hearing is to decide whether I walk out of this courtroom or go back to that jail cell in shackles. If you are going to make that decision today, there's something you desperately need to know."

"Are you sure?" the judge asked.

"No," said Connor.

"Yes," said Ainsley, and she was the more forceful of the two.

"You have one minute," the judge said. "But keep in mind that the only issue I see at this hearing is whether you are a flight risk."

"I understand," said Ainsley. "All I want to say is this: I won't flee because I have no reason to fear these claims against me. Not only am I not guilty, but these allegations are laughable. Supposedly I hooked up with some guy who used my passkey to enter my office and steal my computer. And why did I do that? Because I wanted to steal the code that I created. I repeat:

Code *that I created.* I don't have to steal a computer to get that code. I don't even have to write it down. It's in my head."

The prosecutor rose and shook his head. "Judge, first of all, we're way off track if the court has narrowed the issue at this hearing to risk of flight."

"Perhaps. But it's a very interesting sidetrack."

"Judge, what Ms. Altman just said is so overly simplistic that it borders on quaint. I have no doubt the defendant is a very intelligent young woman, but I've seen this code in written flowchart form. It's an algorithm that runs on for page after page. It's simply beyond the pale to suggest that any normal human being could possibly commit to memory anything so complex and—"

"An integer variable *p*-sub-*i* is defined as the period," said Ainsley, "counted in the number of beacon intervals for host *i* to transmit a beacon, where *p*-sub-*i* equals . . ."

The prosecutor listened with mouth agape as Ainsley continued on, reciting from memory. Behind him, in the first row of public seating, a sudden commotion erupted as the Wall Street lawyers rushed to the rail to get his attention. "Judge, may I have a moment?" asked Goodkin.

"Thirty seconds."

". . . where N is an integer set and NL-sub-*i* is the number of host *i*'s neighbors whose TSF timer is equal to or slower than host *i* . . ."

"Judge, please. Can you tell her to stop?"

"And the value of α is used to adjust the number of hosts to contend for the beacon transmission, where—"

"Judge, come on."

"You can take a breath now, Ms. Altman."

"It's basically a computer time-synchronization algorithm, Your Honor. I can say it backward, if you like. "Power third to the x equals . . ."

"Your Honor, I'm serious. Make her stop."

Judge Larkin seemed almost amused. "That will be all, Ms. Altman."

The prosecutor huddled with the private attorneys at the rail. Connor seized the moment.

"While Mr. Goodkin is circling the Wall Street wagons, Your Honor, I would like to point out that there is legal precedent for the proposition that the court can take into account the apparent weakness of the claims against a defendant in deciding whether the defendant is a flight risk."

"Thank you, Mr. Jameson. Is the prosecution quite ready?"

Goodkin cut the conference short and returned to his place at table. "A couple points, Your Honor. First, even if the defendant has memorized the code she created, it doesn't undermine the claims against her. Our case is premised not only upon the theft of her own code, but also on the theft of existing Hilbert code, which she did not write. Both codes were on the computer that was stolen."

Connor rose. "I don't see that allegation in the existing complaint."

"Neither do I," said the judge.

The prosecutor thumbed through the complaint, searching. "Well, we may need to amend to make that clear, Your Honor. But aside from that, neither the defendant nor anyone else should be reciting proprietary HFT code in open court for public ears. We are here to protect trade secrets, and if the actual code is going to be revealed, we need to clear the courtroom and close these proceedings."

"That won't be necessary at this juncture," the judge said. "I've made my decision. The marshal is directed to return the defendant to the detention center for processing and release. The defendant is free to go on her own recognizance, provided that she remains in the Southern District of New York and surrenders her passport. I'll give the government five days to amend its charges." She banged her gavel. "Next case."

The lawyers on both sides of the courtroom gathered up their materials. Connor, especially, seemed to be in a hurry.

"So I'm free to go without posting bail?" Ainsley asked, whispering.

"Right. Not a dime. The judge trusts you to appear in court based solely on your promise to do so."

"So we totally kicked butt," she said.

"Yeah," he said, but he seemed less than happy. "We did."

The bailiff called the next case. Another lawyer and her client hurried forward and took Connor and Ainsley's place at the defense table. The marshal escorted Ainsley across the courtroom toward the prisoner's exit. She tried to catch Professor Bartow's eye again in the public seating, but the crowd had shuffled in the transition from one case to the next, and Ainsley couldn't spot him. Connor pulled her aside for a word in private before she reached the elevator. Ainsley hadn't seen that annoyed look on his face in quite some time, but she remembered it well enough to know that it wasn't a good sign.

"What's wrong?" she asked.

"I'd almost forgotten how fucking smart you are."

"And you've also forgotten how much I hate pointless overuse of the f-bomb."

"Sorry. Wicked smart. The girl from MIT is wicked smart." He moved closer, as if to underscore the importance of what he needed to say. "But that stunt you just pulled in front of Judge Larkin was the stupidest thing I've ever seen you do."

"It wasn't a stunt. It worked."

"It didn't *work.* You got away with it. Don't ever do it again, or I can't be your lawyer. I hate to be so blunt, but you're my client, and those are my rules. Are we clear?"

"Yeah," she said. "Crystal."

"Good. I have an evidentiary hearing in state court that will last all day. You don't need me for the release from MCC. Let's meet in my office at four-thirty and talk strategy."

"Okay."

He started back toward the courtroom.

"Connor?"

"What?"

"Thank you," she said.

His expression softened, especially around the eyes. With a quick nod he turned and left. Ainsley went to the elevator, her chains rattling as she stepped into the cage.

SEVEN

Ainsley almost kissed the dirty sidewalk. It felt that good to be released from the detention center, even after less than twenty-four hours on the inside. She could only imagine what the feeling might be like after twenty-four months. Or twenty-four years.

I'd be . . . old. A full decade older than her mother had been when she'd told Ainsley good-bye.

She shook off the distressing thought and started toward the subway. A familiar face caught her attention before she got beyond the shadow of the federal courthouse.

"Aloha," said the professor.

The greeting made her smile. Professor Bartow was, without a doubt, one of the smartest people Ainsley had ever met. He was also the flag bearer, so to speak, who carried on the fashion tradition of the former dean of physics, who wore short-sleeved Hawaiian shirts year round no matter how untropical the weather in Cambridge. Hawaii was the focal point of the MIT global telescope project, the very project for which Ainsley had written her much-heralded time-synchronization algorithm. Howard challenged her, pushed her, made her use more of her brainpower than she'd ever thought possible. Sometimes he also made her feel like that little girl in Colorado with such enormous dreams.

I'm going to build the biggest, most amazing telescope in the world.

"Aloha yourself," said Ainsley.

The idea for the world's biggest telescope wasn't Ainsley's or Professor Bartow's. It was a vision shared by scientists who'd looked at the numbers and decided that humans couldn't possibly be alone. The sun is one of four hundred billion stars in the Milky Way galaxy; and even though not all stars have planetary systems, another one hundred billion galaxies out there put the total number of stars at an astounding 10^{22}—which means that, to date, the human search for cosmic company is equivalent to the taking of a single glass of water from the ocean, and no one would conclude that all of the earth's oceans are entirely without life based on the drawing of a single glass of water. The ATA-42 in California was the first telescope built from a large number of small dishes linked by computers, and astrophysicists have been expanding the concept ever since—some with the vision to take it around the globe. The key to a telescope *that* big is an effective time-synchronization algorithm. Time synchronization was also gold to high-frequency traders.

Ainsley wished she had never bridged the two worlds.

"Where you headed?" asked the professor.

"My apartment. I need to talk to my landlord about

extending my lease. The judge said I have to stay in New York until trial."

"I heard that."

"I hope that won't affect my involvement in the project."

"I don't see why it would. I'm pretty sure they have computers and internet in New York. Where would all the gambling and porn addicts be without it?"

"Good point, Professor."

It was chilly in the shadows of Tribeca's iron-façade architecture of another century, which made the professor and his Hawaiian shirt seem even more out of place.

"Didn't you bring a coat?" asked Ainsley.

"I left it on the train."

Typical. Coats, umbrellas, hats—you name it, Professor Bartow had left it on a train, a bus, or God only knows where. Legend had it that Einstein used to get so wrapped up in thought that he once left his house without wearing pants. The professor wasn't quite in that league.

"We'll walk fast," said Ainsley.

Her studio was two blocks away. Ainsley led, and the professor broke into a jog every few steps to keep up. They passed a flower shop and a Jewish bakery on the way. Across the street was a coffeehouse with free Wi-Fi for people who didn't mind sharing personal information with every two-bit hacker in Manhattan. Cambridge and Boston were home to Ainsley, but after a night at the MCC, even the mildly familiar haunts of her temporary neighborhood were comforting.

"You want to come up?" asked Ainsley.

He buried his hands into his pockets, freezing. "I can wait here."

"It's forty-five degrees out here and you're wearing a short-sleeved shirt. Come upstairs."

"Okay, if you insist."

A blast of cold air followed them into the lobby. The elevator was out of order—the third time in the four weeks Ainsley had lived there—so they took the stairwell to the fifth floor. The professor was breathing heavily as they climbed the final flight. Ainsley waited for him to catch up, pushed open the fire door to the hallway, and then froze.

"What's . . . wrong?" he asked, catching his breath.

Ainsley didn't answer. She raced ahead, down the hallway, toward the police officer standing outside her apartment door.

"You can't go inside," the officer said, as he stepped in front of her, blocking her path.

"I live here."

Agent Salazar from the FBI stepped out of her apartment. "We have a search warrant."

Ainsley looked past him. Two other agents were inside. Her apartment was a mess. "A search warrant for what?"

"It's all in the warrant," he said.

She started to read it, then stopped. An agent stepped into the hallway carrying a computer. "Where are you going with that?"

"Excuse me."

"Can somebody please stop and explain what's going on here?"

"Read the court order," said Salazar.

There was an order attached to the warrant. Again, she read quickly:

". . . *the defendant, Ainsley Grace Altman, is hereby prohibited from using the internet from this date until such time as further ordered by the court . . .*"

Ainsley froze. "What kind of a search warrant is this? I can't be shut down like this!"

A second FBI agent emerged from her apartment. He was carrying a laptop.

"Wait," said Ainsley. "Where did that come from?"

"Pardon me, Miss."

"That's not even mine," said Ainsley. "I've never seen that laptop before. I really want to know: *Where* did you get it?"

Professor Bartow watched in silence.

"This is crazy," she said, appealing to Professor Bartow. "I don't even know how that computer got in my apartment, let alone why they have a search warrant for it."

The professor's cell rang. He stepped away and took it. Ainsley took a closer look at the warrant, which appeared to be a separate legal document from the court order. It was a lot of legalese, which was right up her lawyer's alley. She reached for her phone and was about to speed-dial Connor when the professor interrupted.

"I have to get back to Cambridge," he said.

"When?"

"Right now. Federal agents just showed up at the physics department with a search warrant. They're seizing every computer you've ever worked on."

Ainsley went cold. "I'm so sorry about this."

"It's not your fault."

"Thank you for being so understanding. But other folks in the department might not feel the same."

"I'll do what I can."

"Please do. This is spiraling out of control. I can handle everything the FBI is throwing at me, but I don't know what I would do if the department suspends me from the program."

"Don't go there yet. Be strong. I'll call you when I get back to Cambridge."

They said good-bye, and the professor hurried away to the stairwell. Agent Salazar was finishing up the search and appeared to be making his final notations as to the execution of the warrant, which only added to Ainsley's stress: she wanted Connor to come before the FBI left. She speed-dialed his number, but the call went straight to voicemail.

"Please leave a message . . ."

Ainsley didn't know what to say. Professor Bartow's final remark had left her head spinning. It was no overstatement that she could handle anything short of losing her place on Project Cosmic Company. He'd told her "don't go there," but Ainsley was hung up on that one added word:

Yet.

Ainsley gripped the phone tightly, dug deep, and left a message for her lawyer. "Connor, call me. I really need you."

EIGHT

Vladimir took the nonstop from Hong Kong and landed at JFK International Airport at 6:00 p.m. By eight-thirty he was in Rye, New York. It was just him and Marcus Busey, the CEO of White Sands Investments, in the first-floor study of Busey's Tudor-style mansion.

"Brandy?"

"I don't think so," said Vlad. "My internal clock doesn't know if it's time for a shot of caffeine or a snifter of cognac."

Busey filled a glass for himself. By all accounts, Busey was a Wall Street genius, though it was generally recognized that nowhere on earth was the term "genius" thrown around more loosely than on Wall Street, with the possible exception of Hollywood. Busey was always looking for new ways to make money, which was a good thing, because he never ran out of ways to spend it. His ten-acre estate, one of his six homes, was valued at over a hundred million dollars—money well spent if you and your wife needed nine bedrooms, twelve bathrooms, two swimming pools, a clay tennis court, a putting green modeled after the famous twelfth hole at Augusta, a collection of beehives, and three large paddocks. Best of all, Busey had basically stolen the century-old estate in a fire sale from the late Eric Volpe, the disgraced CEO of Saxton Silvers. Busey had snatched up Volpe's helicopter, too, along with a pair of his Bentleys, and even the remnants of Saxton Silvers, a one-time Wall Street icon, which would forever be remembered as the only investment bank that short sellers like Busey had managed to drive into bankruptcy at the height of the subprime crisis. Most investors went "long" on stock, profiting when the company did well; but Busey loved going short, essentially betting that the stock price would decline. He had a knack for making money when others were losing it.

"What's the news from Hong Kong?" asked Busey.

"Sorry, my friend. Nothing is free in this business. Especially information."

Wall Street genius or not, Busey was determined to become a player in the world of high-frequency trading. White Sands had a sizeable HFT division, but Busey had candidly admitted on national television in a CNBC interview that his quants needed to do more if his firm was going to be a leader. Vlad was eager to accommodate—if the price was right. It was the way prop shops like Hilbert operated. The investment banks—too big to fail, too dumb to lead—were constantly on the lookout for a handful of financial whizzes, usually Russian or Chinese, who were on the cutting edge of high-frequency trading. Vlad had aligned Hilbert with four different investment banks in the last two years, moving his team wherever the grass and the money were greener.

Busey took a seat in the leather armchair and faced his guest.

"You'll get your due, Vlad. Tell me."

"Money is about to explode from the Hong Kong Exchange at the speed of light, and I'm holding all the candle power."

"What does that mean?"

"It means that I'm here to talk about something other than Hong Kong. Something I'm actually willing to share with you."

"I'm listening."

"Do you know how many physicists are working for Wall Street high-frequency traders?"

"No idea."

"Thousands. You look inside any firm, you'll find them. The French particle physicist from FERMAT. The Indian Ph.D. in geophysics. But not all physicists are created equal. I found the brain among brainiacs. An astrophysicist working on her Ph.D. at MIT."

"You mean the young woman that you're trying to put in jail?"

"She belongs in jail, but that's beside the point. I still have her algorithm."

"And what is so special about it?"

"She's working on some telescope that's straight out of a Star Trek movie. It's turned her into the go-to person on time-synchronization algorithms. But here's the good part: she used that brainpower to create a time-synchronization algorithm for high-frequency trading—for me."

"Did you come here to brag, or do we have something to talk about?"

"My algorithm is for sale."

Busey tasted his brandy and then rested the snifter on the

table beside him. "What does it do? In simple terms, please."

"It keeps high-frequency traders at firms like White Sands from front-running my stock purchases."

"Front-running is illegal. White Sands doesn't do anything that is against the law."

"David Marcus, who do you think you're talking to? My shop has done four joint ventures in the last year with the biggest firms on Wall Street. I know what you guys do. We taught you how to do it."

"That's an overstatement."

"Only slight. Let's put this in street terms, and I don't mean Wall Street. Think of the prop shops as the crack dealers on the corner. We're your friends for a time. We partner with you, we climb in bed with you, and we teach you just enough about high-frequency trading to get you hooked on the insane profits. Then we come up with something bigger and smarter and so complex that you can't possibly understand it, let alone control it. But here's the key: we can take everything away from you. So now it's time for you to pay. Big."

"That sounds like a threat."

"Business, dude. Business."

"I think you're bluffing. What do you call this new algorithm? Boogey Man?"

"Oh, it's not a bluff. We ran a test before the golden girl was arrested. Penny jumpers were all over my buy orders without the algorithm. Penny jumpers were clueless when we traded with the algorithm. I'm happy to set up a demonstration for you."

"It may come to that. But for discussion purposes, let's assume that it does what you say it does. What do you want?"

"Let's call it a royalty. Ten percent of your HFT profits for the next twelve months."

Busey scoffed, nearly a chuckle. "I'm not giving you ten percent of my profits."

"I didn't mean just White Sands' profits. I want five of the big-boy banks. I don't care which five. Meet with your brethren, and then get back to me."

"That's preposterous."

"You have five days. If we strike a deal, the algorithm remains a trade secret, and you have nothing to fear. If I don't hear from you, I will authorize the U.S. Attorney to reveal my secret in open court in the criminal case against Ainsley Grace Altman. The magic genie will be out of the bottle. Any trader who owns a computer will be able to beat the pants off of you. You and all the other penny jumpers will be fucked."

Busey rose and walked to the credenza by the window. On the wall beside the draperies was a canceled check, yellowed with age, in a gold frame.

"You see this check?" asked Busey.

Vlad squinted to see it. "What about it?"

"It came with the house; I bought it fully furnished from Eric Volpe's estate. This was the first paycheck Eric Volpe earned as a Wall Street trader, long before he went on to be CEO of Saxton and Silvers. Two weeks' pay: six hundred bucks."

Vlad watched but said nothing, not sure where this was headed.

Busey was still staring at the check. "I'm told that Volpe hung it on the wall as a reminder of how far he had come. I keep it there as a reminder of how guys like Volpe crash and burn when they can no longer keep up with a market that's changing all the time. How their charred carcasses are thrown to the wolves and nobody gives a shit. Nobody even cared enough to come into his study and take his framed paycheck down from the wall before selling off his house."

"Does that mean you're in?"

"I can't speak for the others," he said, as he gazed out the window at his well-kept lawn. "But I need to see this thing work with my own eyes."

"I'll set up a demonstration," Vlad said, smiling as he glanced again at the framed memento on the wall. "And bring your checkbook."

NINE

Ainsley caught up with Connor at his law office. The court hearing in his other case had run late, well past the dinner hour, followed by a longer than expected "what the heck is going on" phone conference with the prosecutor in Ainsley's case. It was 9:00 p.m. before he was able to sit down with Ainsley.

"Kung Pau chicken?" he asked. Connor was seated in a high leather chair behind his cluttered desk, poking chopsticks into a cardboard container that, by Ainsley's guesstimate, had probably been sitting in his mini-refrigerator since the weekend. It had been "one of those days," the kind that morphed into a night of cold leftovers.

"I'm not hungry," said Ainsley.

"You have to eat, or the stress will run you into the ground. I've seen clients lose forty, even fifty pounds between arrest and trial."

"I'll grab something really fattening on the way home. Tell me what you and Goodkin talked about."

Connor put down his food and loosened his necktie. Ainsley was in the armchair facing his desk, literally on the edge of her seat.

I wonder how many guilty people have sat in this chair.

"Here's the situation. The FBI—" he started to say, then stopped himself, suddenly aware of the curious expression on Ainsley's face. "What are you looking at?"

The lights were low in Connor's office, and Ainsley had finally noticed the remnants of a black smudge on his forehead. "I guess today is Ash Wednesday?"

"Oh, yeah. I popped into St. Peter's over the lunch break. You're supposed to leave the ashes on all day, but I toned it down a little when I went back to court. Can you still see it?"

"Not at first, but now that I know it's there, it's kind of like a third eye staring back at me."

"You'll get used to it."

It was an innocuous comment, but it landed awkwardly between them. Religion had been a sore spot in their relationship, culminating one night in Boston when Connor had noticed that she was down about something, and she'd told him that it was the anniversary of her mother's death. Meaning well, or perhaps just not knowing what to say or do, Connor invited her to church with him, and she went. The sermon on that Sunday morning had been all about making sense of a nineteen-year-old parishioner who'd driven home from college to visit his parents and was killed by a drunk driver. It was an earnest effort by a good priest, but it sparked a post-service argument between Ainsley and Connor that lasted for hours, then days, and that ultimately blossomed into a fundamental disagreement over how to live their lives and raise children. It was the beginning of the end. Ainsley was no atheist—even Carl Sagan rejected the notion than any living being could "know" there is no God—but she would never warm up to the idea that losing her mother so young was part of a bigger "plan."

But Connor was still one of the good guys.

"You were about to say something about the FBI," said Ainsley.

"Yes. The FBI went to your apartment this afternoon for two reasons."

"Right, the papers that Agent Salazar showed me looked like two different things: a search warrant for a computer, and a court order to keep me off the internet between now and the date of trial."

"Exactly. After the bail hearing, Goodkin went back before the magistrate without us."

"Is that allowed?"

"It's typical for a search warrant. If the FBI has to tip off the other side before their search, the defendant might get rid of the evidence. But I have a problem with the way he got the restraining order."

"It seems to me that if he wanted to keep me off the internet, he should have raised that when we were in front of the judge at the hearing."

"That's exactly right."

"Can we go back and get the judge to cancel the order?"

"'Quash' is the word. Yes. But you'll have to stay off the internet until that happens."

"Then it has to happen fast. I spoke to my faculty advisor. The only way to keep me in the telescope project is if I'm linked by internet while I'm in New York. I don't really understand the prosecutor's concern here anyway. What does he think I'm going to do if I'm online?"

"The theory is that you might do what they allege you were trying to do: sell the code to some third party."

"And the judge bought that argument?"

"For now."

"Do you think you can change her mind?"

"I'm going to try."

"But what if you can't?"

"Then you'll have to stay off the internet until the trial is over."

"How long might that be?"

"We don't have a trial date yet. But it could be several months. At least."

It hit her like a punch to the jaw. "I'll be toast."

"We'll figure out a way for you to do your work. At the very least, the judge should let you access the internet with some level of monitoring by a pretrial services officer."

"You're joking, right? They're going to monitor my internet activity, as if I'm no more trustworthy than a sex offender?

"That's the worst-case scenario."

"It's ridiculous."

Her lawyer didn't disagree, but he didn't say it wouldn't happen, either. "Let's talk about the search warrant," said Connor.

Ainsley had a copy in front of her. "This is even more bizarre. I don't even own the laptop listed in this search warrant, but somehow the FBI agent found it in my apartment and walked out the door with it."

"The laptop belongs to Hilbert Trading Group. The search warrant relates to the amended charges that the government mentioned at the bail hearing: You didn't just steal the code you created; you stole existing HFT code that was proprietary to Hilbert. I presume that the proprietary code was on this computer."

"I *never* took a laptop home from Hilbert."

"Then how did it get in your apartment?"

"This is a setup. Someone put it there. The same way they bought that plane ticket to Taiwan under my name."

"Who?"

"I don't know. It could be anyone who works at Hilbert. The prosecutor kept saying that *I* have a serious motive to sell my algorithm to competitors who could use it to manipulate the market. The fact is, everyone at Hilbert has that same motive."

"That's true. But it's not easy to prove that you're being framed."

"We have to prove it."

"No. We don't have to prove anything. We're the defense. The burden of proof is on the government to prove its case beyond a reasonable doubt."

"I understand your point. But my defense is that I'm being framed."

"That's one of your defenses."

"What else do I have?"

"I'll get to that. But first, let's take a step back and consider your options in the broadest sense. In all likelihood, we will see an indictment in the next couple days with the new charges. The next thing is your arraignment. You have to enter a plea: guilty or not guilty."

"That's a no-brainer."

"Well, let's talk about that. Before I hung up the phone with Goodkin, he made overtures toward a plea bargain. I think there's a possibility that he would recommend probation, no jail time, if . . ."

"If what?"

"If you name your accomplice."

"My accomplice?"

"The guy who stole the computer from your office at Hilbert Trading."

"Whoa. Have I not been clear about this? There is no accomplice."

"Don't be offended by my thoroughness. I'm your lawyer."

"Do you think I did this?"

He didn't answer. Ainsley rose—sprang, actually—from her chair. She went to the window and stared out at the massive high-rise across the street from Connor's tiny office, measuring her words before speaking. Then she turned around and faced her lawyer. "You don't believe I'm innocent, do you?"

"It doesn't matter if I do or not."

"It matters *to me.*"

He drew a breath. "Look, Ainsley."

"Connor, you can forget cutting a deal with Goodkin. I'm not pleading guilty to something I didn't do."

"I'm not saying you're guilty."

"But you can't say I'm innocent? Is that it?"

"What I'm saying is that your guilt or innocence is between you and God, you and your conscience, you and whatever metaphysical particles you connect with. But it makes no difference to me as your lawyer."

Her comment about the ash and the third eye had obviously bugged him, but she chose not to go down that road. "Connor, hear what I'm saying. I don't know who stole that computer from my office, and I wasn't working with anybody to steal my own code. I'm not looking for an argument with you, but I have to say this: I can't have a lawyer who doesn't believe what I tell him."

Again Connor said nothing, or at least he didn't speak fast enough to suit Ainsley.

"Connor, do you believe me?"

Another deep breath, and then his response: "Yes. I believe you."

Silence hung in the air, until Ainsley broke it. "Good. I'm glad that's settled."

"I just want to say one thing."

"Say it. This is no time to tap dance around my feelings. I want you to say exactly what's on your mind."

"I know. But this is hard for me, since we're old friends."

Old friends. There it was again. "We have to put that aside. In fact, Professor Bartow is looking into whether MIT will pay my legal bill, and if they don't, I'll pay you somehow. So this isn't even technically a favor for an old friend."

"No, I wasn't talking about my fee arrangement. What I'm trying to get across is that you're not the first innocent client I've ever represented. And you wouldn't be the first to enter a guilty plea in exchange for no jail time."

"You actually let an innocent person plead guilty?"

"I know that must sound awful. But an offer of no jail time might not be on the table next month or even next week. It's something to consider, especially when you're looking at twenty-five years in federal prison, if convicted. A plea bargain is a calculated risk."

"I'm well aware of the downside. We simply have to beat this, Connor."

"I know."

"I think the correct answer is 'we will'."

He nodded, but it wasn't in full agreement. "It's good for you to stay positive. But I never make that promise to any client. I wish I could make it to you. But I can't."

"I understand." She checked her watch. "I'm really tired. I didn't sleep at all last night."

"I'm not surprised. Why don't we pick this up in the morning?"

They agreed on 7:00 a.m., before Connor had to be in court on another case. Ainsley grabbed her coat and purse.

"I'll walk you out," said Connor.

It was all of twenty feet to the door. His office suite was only slighter larger than Ainsley's studio, and he suddenly seemed embarrassed about it.

"I guess you could have found your way without my help," he said.

"It's okay."

"I've been looking for a bigger place, but rents are pretty brutal."

"Hey, it's not where you start. It's where you finish."

He offered a cathartic smile. "That's what they say."

Their eyes met and held for a moment, until that third one caught Ainsley's attention again.

"Good night, Cyclops."

He took it with a sense of humor and opened the door.

"Cyclops had one eye, not three."

"It's the holy trinity of Cyclops. Three equals one." Ainsley started out.

"Hey," he said, stopping her.

"What?"

"For what it's worth, I lit a candle for you today at St. Peter's."

"Thanks," she said, nodding her appreciation. "That was nice of you."

Then she turned and started toward the elevator.

TEN

"Absolutely not guilty, Your Honor," said Ainsley.

The indictment had come down even sooner than expected: two counts of theft of trade secrets in violation of the Economic Espionage Act. On Thursday morning Ainsley was back in Judge Larkin's courtroom to enter a plea. Two rows of the press seating section were completely filled, more than double the media turnout for her bail hearing. The number of spectators in public seating had also grown, but this time, she noted, there was no Hawaiian shirt in the back row. On the plus side, at least she wasn't wearing prison garb and shackles.

"A simple 'not guilty' will suffice," the judge said.

Obviously Judge Larkin would not have been a fan of the screen saver on Ainsley's computer back at MIT: *Anything Worth Doing Is Worth Overdoing. Anything Worth Doing Is Worth Overdoing.*

Connor stepped forward. "Judge, I have one other issue I'd like to raise with the court at this time."

Ainlsey's pulse quickened. Connor had warned her that the judge might move them along with no opportunity to say anything beyond "not guilty." The "other issue," however, was by far the more important one.

"What is it, Mr. Jameson?"

Ainsley wished she could speak, but she could only listen and hope as Connor explained the need to the dissolve the restraining order that would keep her from doing her research. "Judge, this order was obtained *ex parte*, without any opportunity for the defense to be heard on the matter. We raised no objection at the bail hearing to the court's requirement that Ms. Altman remain in New York pending trial. But keeping my client off the internet between now and trial will effectively cut her off from the physics department at MIT, which is an extreme and unnecessary hardship."

"I understand," the judge said. "This is a *temporary* restraining order that I entered to address the government's immediate concerns. I will revisit the issue as soon as I can set aside time for a full evidentiary hearing."

Ainsley nudged her lawyer, and Connor took her cue. "We'd like that hearing to take place immediately, Your Honor."

The prosecutor rose. "Judge, if may interject. The concerns expressed by the government in our application for the restraining order are very real. As the two-count indictment makes clear, the defendant is charged not only with stealing the code that she created, but also the firm's existing high-frequency trading code that her new program was supposed to enhance, and which Hilbert Trading Group invested millions of dollars to create."

"Which raises another important issue," said Connor. "The entire justification for the order that keeps my client off the internet is that she has allegedly stolen trade secrets and that she might sell them to third parties."

"That's a legitimate concern in any trade secret case," said the prosecutor.

"Yes," said Connor, "but only after the government has proven that what they are trying to protect is, in fact, a trade secret."

The judge did a double take. "Mr. Jameson, are you making the argument that these high-frequency trading codes are not proprietary to Hilbert Trading Group and are not trade secrets?"

"That's the precise argument I want the opportunity to make," said Connor.

Ainsley glanced in the prosecutor's direction. The incredulous expression on his face mirrored his reaction to Ainsley's verbatim recitation of her time-synchronization algorithm at the bail hearing.

"Judge, the very idea that these codes are not trade secrets is preposterous. Hilbert has spent millions and millions—"

"There he goes again," said Connor. "I keep hearing the millions and millions of dollars argument. But the indictment makes nothing more than a bald assertion that the codes are trade secrets. The government's application for the restraining order also referenced the theft of codes that my client did not create, but it doesn't give us a clue about what the actual codes are."

"Those codes are trade secrets," said Goodkin. "The government should not be required to reveal the actual codes in order to prosecute someone for stealing them. That's absurd."

"The government has to reveal them to the defense," said Connor. "I need to have an independent expert evaluate those codes. If my expert concludes that there is nothing proprietary about these codes, I am allowed to put that expert on the witness stand to testify that they are not trade secrets. If they are not trade secrets, no crime has been committed."

The Hilbert lawyers rushed to the rail. It tickled Ainsley to see them in such acute distress as they struggled to get the prosecutor's attention.

"Judge, may I have a moment?" asked Goodkin.

"No. This isn't the time for this, but I do think Mr. Jameson has a point. We will reconvene this afternoon at three p.m. The government should be prepared to establish that the additional high-frequency trading codes referenced in the indictment are trade secrets. We can sort out what precautions are necessary to protect the alleged secrets from public disclosure at that time. That's all for now."

"Thank you, Your Honor," said Connor.

Ainsley took another look across the courtroom where the prosecutor and the Wall Street lawyers had huddled in privacy. The lead lawyer was speaking in rapid-fire fashion, the very thought of having to reveal his client's HFT secrets pushing him to the brink of cardiac arrest.

"Yes," Ainsley said quietly. "Thank you so much, Judge."

ELEVEN

"A pox on your penny-jumping houses," said Vladimir. He hit ENTER on his keyboard and placed an electronic order for ten thousand shares of stock at \$36.07 per share. Just five minutes earlier, the same order had been intercepted in cyberspace by the high-frequency-trading algorithms of at least five different firms. Each time, in the blink of an eye, the winning algorithm had tried to sell the stock to him at \$36.08, a penny more than he was willing to pay. This time, his order sailed right through at his price.

"It works," said Busey.

Vlad was alone in his corner office with the CEO of White Sands. This was the "see it with my own eyes" demonstration that Busey had demanded at their first meeting at Busey's mansion. The expression on the banker's face was as priceless as the algorithm that Vladimir was trying to sell him.

"How on earth did she do that?" asked Busey, meaning Ainsley.

"First of all, I have no idea. But even if I could explain it, I wouldn't. All you need to know is that if I go public with this trading algorithm, I can put an end to the penny-jumping profits of every investment bank on Wall Street."

Busey was still staring at the trading screen in disbelief, but Vlad could practically read his mind. Busey was president of an institution that derived forty percent of its annual revenue and seventy percent of its profit from its most risky and volatile line of business: trading and investing. Even in bull markets, the firm's trading desk spent forty days a year operating in the red. In other words, White Sands's investment banking division could arrange the biggest deals in town, its asset management division could manage client portfolios with precision, and one boneheaded call by a single group of traders could still land the entire firm in the toilet. That was the beauty of penny jumping. At long last, investment banks had some level of *guaranteed* profits incorporated into the bottom line.

One algorithm created by one smart astrophysicist could bring it all to an abrupt end.

There was a knock at the door. Only Vladimir's trusted assistant would have the nerve to interrupt a meeting like this one. "What is it, Martha?"

The door opened and his assistant poked her head into the office. "Jake Sizemore is on the line. He says it's urgent."

Sizemore was the lead Wall Street lawyer monitoring the criminal prosecution against Ainsley Altman. Vlad excused himself and stepped into the private conference room that was part of his multi-room office suite. He kept an eye on Busey through the wall of beveled glass as he spoke in private to his lawyer.

"What is it, Jake?"

His lawyer told him about that morning's developments in court before Judge Larkin. Vlad grasped the urgency: "So you're saying that we have to prove that these algorithms are trade secrets?"

"That's where it stands now. The prosecutor asked me to identify the best witness at Hilbert who can provide this testimony."

"The best witness is *me*," said Vlad. "But this is bullshit. If Hilbert is going to reveal these codes, it will be on my terms. Not because Little Miss Brainsley and her lawyer demand it."

"I understand. But we won't be in any position to dictate our own terms if the judge orders it."

"Then make sure she doesn't order it."

"In the worst case," said the lawyer, "the judge will force you to disclose it only after closing the courtroom to the public. And the transcript would be sealed."

"I don't care what protections the judge comes up with. I don't want these codes released to the judge, to the prosecutor, or to anyone else unless I say it's okay to release them."

"That's why this afternoon's hearing is so important. Are you available?"

Vlad hesitated. "Give me a minute. I'll check."

He put his lawyer on hold, stepped out of the conference room, and returned to his desk. But he didn't check his calendar. He looked Busey in the eye and said, "I need an answer. Are you buying the algo?"

"I'm interested. But let's talk about the price."

"The price is not negotiable. Ten percent of all HFT profits for twelve months."

"How do you expect me to justify a number that big?"

"I'm not asking you to dip into a slush fund to make an illegal payment. This is a legitimate business expense. Think of it like the pay-for-delay settlements in the drug industry."

The analogy was tailor-made for Busey. Vlad knew that White Sands had raked in a ton of money by investing in pharmaceutical companies that paid competing manufacturers to keep less expensive generic brands from coming onto the market.

"Pay for delay is illegal," said Busey.

"So is jaywalking, but it doesn't keep people in the crosswalk when it's more expedient to step outside the lines."

"I can only speak for White Sands today. I haven't met with any of the other firms."

"I need to know everyone is in."

Busey shifted uneasily in his chair. "I need more time."

"I don't have time to give you. I'm taking the witness stand this afternoon."

"I can't have an answer by then."

"Then ante up for the others. Ten percent from the big five. Pledge fifty percent of your HFT profits and collect from the others later."

"Have you lost your mind?"

"No. Take another look at your books and see what you make from penny jumping every year. Then imagine my algorithm going public and erasing all that cash flow."

"But—"

"No buts. Fifty percent of something is better than a hundred percent of nothing. What's it going to be, Busey? You good for it, or do I walk into federal court this afternoon, let the genie named Ainsley out of the bottle, and shut down all you penny jumpers? My lawyer is on hold waiting for an answer."

Busey drew a breath, and then glanced through the beveled glass toward the telephone's blinking light on the conference room table. His gaze shifted back to Vlad.

And then he gave his answer.

TWELVE

At 3:00 p.m. Ainsley was back in court, the Honorable Judge Shelley Larkin presiding.

"Is the government ready to proceed?" the judge asked.

Goodkin rose, buttoned his suit coat, and stepped toward the microphone at the lectern. "Your Honor, the government of course welcomes this opportunity to prove that the codes stolen by the defendant are trade secrets. Our best witness on this issue is Vladimir Kosov, president and CEO of Hilbert Trading Group. Unfortunately, Mr. Kosov was suddenly called away on an urgent business matter."

"Called away to where?" the judge asked.

"Hong Kong."

"Then put on your second-best witness," the judge said.

"That's not as easy as it sounds," said the prosecutor. "Hilbert is an international proprietary stock trading firm with offices and traders around the globe. Mr. Kosov is the only one of the five principals who is actually based in New York. The others are in Moscow. I've done the best I can to have a witness here today, Your Honor. But there's only so much I can do in three hours."

"Are you asking for a continuance of the hearing?" the judge asked.

"Yes, Your Honor."

The judge looked at Connor. "Let me hear from the defense."

Ainsley grabbed her lawyer by the sleeve and filled his ear with her thoughts. Connor nodded once before he rose, confirming that he was on the same page.

"Judge, clearly my client would be prejudiced by the delay of this hearing, since every day she is kept off the internet puts her that much further behind on her research at MIT. However, the defense will agree to reschedule this hearing to a date after Mr. Kosov returns from Hong Kong on two conditions. One: the government agrees to lift the restriction on my client's use of the internet. Two: my client is allowed to travel once a week between New York City and Cambridge, Massachusetts."

"Number one is agreeable," said the prosecutor. "Number two is out of the question."

"Internet access and travel rights are granted," the judge said. "My previous bail order is so amended. Next time you come to a hearing in my courtroom, Mr. Goodkin, come prepared. We are adjourned."

The judge ended it with a crack of her gavel. All rose on the bailiff's familiar command. The courtroom froze in silence until Judge Larkin disappeared through the side door to her chambers. Then a commotion took over, but mostly on the prosecutor's side of the courtroom. Members of the media rushed to the rail for a quote from one of the lawyers. Connor ignored the clamor behind them in the public seating, keeping his voice down as he spoke to his client.

"This couldn't have played out better," Connor whispered. "I think we've pushed the right button by raising this trade secret issue."

"I don't buy it for a moment that Mr. Kosov was suddenly called out on business."

"Nor do I. Hilbert is very uncomfortable with the prospect of revealing these codes, even if the courtroom is closed to the public."

"Clearly they have something to hide," said Ainsley. "And I don't just mean the codes themselves. I may be overly optimistic, but my gut tells me that if this keeps up, their top priority won't be to put me in jail for stealing their codes. It will be to keep the world from finding how they intend to use them."

"That's my strategy. I'm betting that Hilbert would sooner tell the U.S. Attorney to drop this prosecution than reveal its secrets."

"Thank you, Connor. Just getting back in touch with the physics department is such a weight off my shoulders."

"You're welcome," he said as he reached for his briefcase. "I set aside the rest of the afternoon for this hearing, so my calendar is completely clear. Should we head over to O'Malley's and have a celebratory pint?"

"Sorry. No time. I need to run."

"Where?"

"Penn Station," she said. "I have a train to catch. To Boston."

THIRTEEN

Ainsley's train reached Boston that evening, and she rode the subway under the river and into Cambridge. A cool night greeted her as she emerged from the Kendall Square Station. She felt safe walking alone in this area after dark, even as she passed the memorial to Sean Collier, the MIT police officer gunned down at this intersection by the Boston Marathon bombers. From there it was a fifteen-minute walk to the heart of campus and the famous domed library on Killian Court. Designed by John D. Rockefeller's personal architect, the dome atop the classic stone columns of Building 10, together with Maclaurin Buildings 3 and 4, formed an impressive "U" on three sides of the court. This protected and picturesque green space, facing the Charles River, would be the site of Ainsley's commencement exercise upon completion of her doctoral program.

Unless I'm in prison.

Ainsley walked quickly past Maclaurin 3, which she hadn't set foot in since day one on campus, when a colleague introduced himself as "Helpful Albert" and told her that Professor Bartow wanted to meet with her in Room 3-369. It turned out to be the lactation room. Ainsley had been quick to even the score. In a show of teamwork that proved they could be friends after the breakup, Connor posed as a television producer and offered to fly Albert to LA as a paid consultant for an episode of *The Big Bang Theory*. Albert was on his way to Logan International when Ainsley called and told him that the airline ticket was a fake and that the gig was a gag.

Ainsley entered Maclaurin 4, home to the physics department, and climbed the stairwell to Professor Bartow's office. She'd phoned him several times since leaving New York and reached only his voice mail, which was normal. When the professor was in his think zone, there was no penetrating his intellectual cocoon. Ainsley was about to knock on his office door, on which Professor Bartow had posted his saying of the day: "*I Don't Trust Atoms. They Make Up Everything.*" But she stopped. Something was noticeably different about the large bulletin board on the wall outside his office. It displayed a photograph and bio for each team member on Project Cosmic Company. Ainsley's had been removed.

"Ainsley?"

She turned and saw Professor Bartow standing behind her, a fresh cup of coffee in his hand.

"Why are my picture and bio down?" she asked.

"What are you doing out of New York?"

She quickly explained Judge Larkin's modification of her bail conditions and then repeated her question.

"Let's talk in my office," he said.

She followed him inside and closed the door. He cleared away a towering stack of academic journals from a chair so Ainsley could sit, and then he settled into his desk chair.

"You're not wearing a Hawaiian shirt," said Ainsley. It was an odd start to the conversation, but never had Ainsley seen him wear anything else. Professor Bartow in a black sweater was an image that just didn't compute.

"It's my sign of protest."

"What are you protesting?"

He looked away, then back. "I've been struggling with this all day, trying to figure out how to tell you. This morning, the department voted to suspend you from the program."

Ainsley didn't move, but it felt like a mule kick. "Why?"

"Ainsley, not to state the obvious, but you've been indicted for stealing trade secrets."

"I didn't do it."

"That was my argument at the department meeting, but it didn't carry the day."

Ainsley tried to breathe. It wasn't easy. "Is it the press coverage? Is the department afraid of the bad publicity?"

"That hasn't helped. But in my opinion, what tipped the scale against you was the FBI showing up here at the department with a search warrant. It covered every computer you've ever worked on."

"It makes me so angry that the government overreached like that. My work at Hilbert had nothing to do with my research here."

"You're right. Which leads to more bad news."

"What could be worse?"

"Because the two are unrelated, the department will not be paying your legal bills in the criminal case. I'm sorry."

She nodded slowly, not in agreement, but simply to acknowledge the size of her problems. "I'll have to tell Connor."

"I wish there was something I could do."

"Are you the only one on my side?"

"You know I can't tell you how the department's vote broke down."

"Exactly what are the terms of my suspension?"

He pulled an envelope from his desk drawer and handed it to her. "It's all spelled out in here. You need to read this, sign it, and return it to me."

She stared at the envelope, then tucked it into her purse without opening it. Her gaze shifted toward the huge map of the world, which covered an entire wall. Above it were the words "Project Cosmic Company." It was the global telescope, and red dots across the map marked each location of its component parts. The Atacama Desert in Chile, the highest desert in the world. The eucalyptus woodlands in New South Wales, Australia. The volcano of Mauna Kea on the Big Island in Hawaii. The Grenadines in the southern Caribbean Sea. These and other strategic locations would be linked together by supercomputers, their operations time-synchronized in accordance with Ainsley's algorithm to bring a childhood dream to life.

I'm going to create the biggest, most amazing telescope in the world.

"It's over for me, isn't it?"

He folded his hands atop his desk, unable to look her in the eye. "I'm sorry, Ainsley. I should never have approved your application to work for Hilbert. I should have protected you from these Wall Street barracudas. This would never have happened."

"That's not your fault."

"I let you down. I feel like I've let your mother down. She and I were so close, and I—"

"It's okay."

"No, it's not okay. I'm going to keep fighting. I don't care if I never wear another Hawaiian shirt as long as I live. I will protest, I will fight, and we will win."

Ainsley tried to smile, but it wouldn't come. "Yes, we will," she said in a voice that faded.

FOURTEEN

Wednesday was a tough night. Ainsley read and reread the terms of her suspension. Nothing short of complete vindication in a court of law would save her.

Thursday was a day for travel to New York, reflection, and preparation. On Friday afternoon, it was show time. Vladimir Kosov was back from Hong Kong. Ainsley was before Judge Larkin on a preliminary hearing. There was no jury. It was the prosecutor's burden to demonstrate to a judge that the charges were supported by sufficient evidence to proceed to trial. It was the defendant's opportunity to poke holes in the government's case.

"The United States of America calls Vladimir Kosov," said the prosecutor.

Kosov didn't so much as cut his eyes at Ainsley as he approached the stand. The bailiff swore the witness. Observers in public seating sat up and took notice. Members of the media readied their tablets, iPads, pens, and notepads. The government had made no request to close the courtroom, which told Ainsley that Kosov would assiduously avoid specifics in his testimony about codes.

The prosecutor stepped forward, his tone conversational. "Mr. Kosov, please give us a quick background on the development of high-frequency-trading computer code at Hilbert."

"Certainly. Over a period of years, Hilbert has devoted substantial resources to developing and maintaining a computer platform that allows us to engage in sophisticated, high-speed, and high-volume trades on stock and commodities markets."

Ainsley tried not to roll her eyes. *Boy, that didn't sound rehearsed at all.*

"In a broad sense, how does your platform operate?"

"It's about speed and efficiency. In a matter of milliseconds, our platform obtains and processes information about market developments. Additional programs using sophisticated mathematical formulas then kick in—again I'm talking milliseconds—to place automated trades based on the latest market conditions."

"Is this profitable for your firm?"

"Naturally. We're in business to make money."

"There must be costs associated with it."

"Millions of dollars," he said. "That's why we treat the platform, programs, and the underlying computer code to be confidential and proprietary."

"Let's talk about how you protect your investment. What restrictions do you place on employee access to computer codes?"

"All employees, including consultants like Ms. Altman, are prohibited from transmitting code outside of our computer network. They also sign detailed confidentiality and nondisclosure agreements."

"What internal steps has Hilbert taken to prevent the unauthorized transfer of code?"

"So many things. For example, we scan outgoing e-mail messages to prevent the unauthorized transfer of code. We also prohibit FTP file transfers outside of our network."

"Do you also prohibit employees from walking out the door with desktop computers?"

"Objection," said Connor.

"Overruled. The witness may answer."

"That goes without saying. Yes."

The prosecutor continued. "Does Hilbert have security measures in place to restrict physical access to the building? I don't mean locks on the doors. I mean restrictions on employee access."

"Employees and consultants are issued cards that must be swiped in an electronic sensor."

"Did Ms. Altman have a card?"

"She was actually issued two passkeys. The first one was reported missing by Ms. Altman. She was then issued a new card. The old one was deactivated."

"Was that lost card used at any time after Ms. Altman reported it missing?"

"Yes. It was reactivated by . . ." he paused, as if sensing that Connor was about to jump up and object. "By someone. Then it was used to enter the building on the night the desktop computer assigned to Ms. Altman was stolen."

"Let's talk about laptop computers owned by Hilbert. Are employees and consultants allowed to take laptops home?"

"Only with prior authorization."

"You're aware that a Hilbert laptop was retrieved from Ms. Altman's apartment, are you not?"

"Yes, I am."

"Was she authorized to take that laptop home?"

"No."

"Were any programs and codes that you described actually on the laptop computer that was found in Ms. Altman's apartment?"

"Yes, there were."

"Were any programs or codes actually on the desktop computer that was removed from her office?"

"Yes, there were."

The prosecutor stepped away to check his notes, then returned. "Just a couple more questions to wrap things up, Mr. Kosov. Do these proprietary codes afford Hilbert any competitive advantage over other firms that also engage in high-volume automated trading?"

"Without question."

"What would happen to that competitive advantage if the codes were disclosed?"

"We'd lose it. Period. Even worse, if the codes fell into the wrong hands, the market could be manipulated in ways that are beyond the imaginative powers of the human mind. That's especially true with respect to the code created by Ms. Altman."

"Thank you, Mr. Kosov. That's all I have." The prosecutor returned to his seat at the table.

"Cross-examination?" the judge asked.

Connor rose, thanked the judge, and approached the witness. It suddenly occurred to Ainsley that she had never seen her lawyer cross-examine a witness. Her gut told her that he wouldn't disappoint.

"I heard you mention a lot of secret codes, Mr. Kosov. I didn't hear you mention any patents on those codes. Do you have any?"

He seemed puzzled by the question. "No. We've never applied for any."

"How about copyrights? Got any of those to protect your secret codes and programs?"

"No. Never applied."

"So if I plucked one of those secret algorithms from cyberspace, it wouldn't say 'patent pending' on the label, would it?"

"Asked and answered," said the prosecutor. "He already said they never applied."

"Sustained. You made your point, Mr. Jameson."

Connor moved on. "Now, Mr. Kosov, you would agree with me that not every trading algorithm in the world is a trade secret."

Kosov hesitated, as if to make sure he wasn't being tricked. "It's not a secret unless you protect the codes, if that's your point."

"Exactly. In fact, there are some sophisticated trading algorithms that started out as secrets, but they are now very well known throughout the industry. Isn't that right, sir?"

"I would say yes, that's true."

"You guys in the high-frequency trading business are decoding each other's algorithms all the time, aren't you?"

"I don't know about that."

"Oh, come on, Mr. Kosov. Are you telling me that Hilbert has never attempted to unravel the trading algorithm of one of its competitors?"

The prosecutor rose. "Objection, Judge."

"Overruled."

"I can't recall anything specific," said the witness.

Connor went to the projector, and Ainsley knew what was coming. She'd prepared him thoroughly, and his explanation to the judge was faithful to her coaching. "Judge, algorithms can be expressed in different ways. Some are written in computer programming language or in pseudocode, others are in mathematical formulas, and so on. I'd like to show the witness a few trading algorithms expressed in graph format."

"Go right ahead."

At the push of a button, an image flashed on the screen. It resembled a series of striated bars on a decibel meter. "Mr. Kosov, have you heard of a trading algorithm called the Boston Shuffler?"

"That one is very widely known, yes."

"It's a penny-jumper trading algo, correct?"

"That's correct."

"Does Hilbert have a penny-jumper trading algorithm?"

"Yes."

"How does your algorithm differ from this one?"

"That's not my area of expertise. I couldn't tell you."

Connor moved to the next exhibit. A new image flashed on the screen. The bars in the image were similar to the depiction of the Boston Shuffler, but there were more peaks and valleys, and it was in brighter colors. "Here's another trading algorithm. It's called Carnival. Have you heard of this one?"

"Everyone in the business has heard of Carnival."

"Carnival is not a penny jumper, is it?"

"No. It's what the industry calls a 'tow-the-iceberg' algorithm."

"Let's not bother with the details of what 'tow the iceberg' means in the world of high-frequency trading. But does Hilbert have a 'tow the iceberg' trading algorithm?"

"Yes. Everyone does."

"How does it differ from Carnival?"

"Like I said, I don't have that level of technical expertise. I can't tell you precisely."

Connor switched off the projector and stepped toward the witness. "Mr. Kosov, for all you know, Hilbert created its penny jumper and iceberg algorithms by borrowing code straight from the programs I just showed you. Isn't that possible?"

"I highly doubt it."

"But you don't know for sure, do you?"

"I can't say with precision how they differ."

"So, the code that my client is accused of stealing from Hilbert could be identical to Carnival, the Boston Shuffler, and other publicly available trading algorithms, right?"

"Objection," said Goodkin. "That question calls for complete speculation."

"Judge, the point is that if anything in this courtroom is 'complete speculation,' it's the allegations against my client."

"Overruled. The witness may answer."

"Hilbert pays its people very well," said Kosov. "They wouldn't just borrow code that's publicly available and then charge me as if it were their own creation."

"So that's your position: because you paid a lot of money, your algorithms are trade secrets?"

"Objection. Argumentative."

"I'll sustain the objection," the judge said. "But to be honest, the question isn't a totally unfair characterization of the witness's testimony. It's your burden, Mr. Goodkin, to prove that these codes are trade secrets. So far, I've heard nothing but generalities and a lot of huffing and puffing about how much money Hilbert spent and how much it makes."

"We have additional evidence, Judge," said Goodkin.

"Let's hope so."

Connor stepped away and did a final check with Ainsley at the table. "Anything I'm forgetting?" he asked quietly.

Ainsley whispered one suggestion. Even as a non-lawyer, she knew it wasn't an entirely appropriate question, and she could see from Connor's reaction that he would be slapped down for asking it. But they came to a silent agreement that it was worth a shot.

"Your Honor, just one final line of questioning," said Connor.

"Proceed."

"Mr. Kosov, you said that these trading algorithms, especially the one created by my client, could be used to manipulate the market if they fell into the wrong hands."

"Yes. I totally believe that's true."

"I'm curious: How can we be sure that *yours* are the *right* hands?"

"Objection!"

"Sustained. Now you are arguing with the witness, Mr. Jameson."

"Sorry, Your Honor. I think that'll do it. No further questions."

Connor returned to his chair beside Ainsley. She would have high-fived him if she could have, but he quickly brought the astrophysicist back to earth.

"Just the first inning," he said softly. "It's a long ball game."

FIFTEEN

An hour into the hearing, Judge Larkin announced a thirty-minute recess. The prosecution and defense remained in the courtroom to prepare for the next witness. Vladimir headed straight for the rear exit, ignoring the gaggle of reporters and flurry of questions that trailed him and his team of lawyers down the long corridor. They retreated to an empty jury room to talk strategy behind closed doors.

"They are kicking our ass," said Vladimir as he took a seat at the head of the rectangular table. His lawyers—five of them—filled in the remaining chairs.

"It wasn't as bad as you think," said Sizemore.

Jake Sizemore was the silver-haired senior partner on the case. Vladimir was losing patience with him. This wasn't Moscow, but in Vladimir's book, any lawyer who charged a thousand dollars an hour and couldn't buy a judge should have the decency to find some other way to deliver the goods.

"I was a punching bag on that witness stand," said Vladimir. "Clearly Mr. Jameson's strategy is to get Judge Larkin to rule that this prosecution cannot go forward unless I testify in detail about all of the trading algorithms that we claim were stolen."

"That's why I'm not worried," said Sizemore. "That's not the law. If the judge sides with the defense on this, the government will win on appeal."

"I'm not interested in winning on appeal. I'm a microsecond away from closing a nine-figure deal with five investment banks who are all scared shitless that Ainsley's algorithm might go public. If this judge forces my hand—if I lose control over the power to reveal or conceal that algorithm—I lose all leverage to make that deal happen."

Sizemore shifted uncomfortably. "Be careful, Vladimir. I'm not going to say it sounds like extortion, but with the U.S. Attorney's office so closely involved, you want to avoid even the slightest scent of it."

"I don't need my lawyer to tell me how to negotiate. I need just one thing from you, Jake. Get the prosecutor to play his smoking gun."

"Vladimir, today is just a preliminary hearing. All the government has to do is show the judge that there is sufficient evidence for the case to proceed to trial. Goodkin will not want to tip his hand and lay out his strongest evidence now. It's not good strategy."

"I don't give a shit about his strategy. I need this circus to end. The quickest way to shut down all this legal nonsense about whether or not my codes are trade secrets is to show the judge that Ainsley is a thief. Tell Goodkin to pull the trigger."

"Okay. If that's what you want, I'll talk to Goodkin. I'll do my best."

"No. I don't want your best. I need results. Your job is to get the prosecutor to launch his nuclear weapon and end this hearing with a bang. If you can't get Goodkin to do that, tell me now, so I can fire you."

Sizemore locked eyes with his client. Kosov stared right back at him. The lawyer was the first to blink. "All right, Vlad. I'll get it done."

SIXTEEN

A nervous feeling crept over Ainsley as the prosecutor rose to call his next witness.

Goodkin had disappeared from the courtroom for the final fifteen minutes of the recess. Ainsley had a pretty firm guess where he'd gone. She wasn't ready to say that Vladimir's lawyers were running the show, but she had the distinct impression that they were at the very least the executive producers.

"The United States of America calls FBI Special Agent Michael Salazar," said Goodkin.

Maybe even the casting directors.

Salazar raised his right hand, swore to tell the truth, and took a seat in the witness box, which quickly added to Ainsley's anxiety. She had always thought of herself as an honest person. Yet, there she was in a federal courthouse and a federal agent was about to tell a federal judge why she belonged in a federal prison.

"Please introduce yourself to the court, Agent Salazar."

Ainsley listened as Salazar laid out his background and

credentials, which were impressive. A Juris Doctorate from Fordham Law School. More than a decade of experience in the FBI, mostly with the securities fraud unit at the New York field office. And he spoke with such confidence. Ainsley would have believed him, if she were the judge.

"Agent Salazar, I understand that you are overseeing this entire investigation. For purposes of this preliminary hearing, however, I want to focus on one specific aspect of it."

"Okay."

Okay, thought Ainsley. *What is it?*

"Let's talk about what the FBI found on the computers that were searched at the Department of Physics at MIT in Cambridge."

Ainsley's heart sank. Her best hope to overturn her suspension was to convince the judge and her department that her research at MIT was irrelevant to her criminal case. Goodkin was apparently determined to tie the two together.

"Objection," said Connor, rising. "The defense has not yet seen the results of that search."

"It looks like we're all about to," the judge said. "Overruled."

The prosecutor continued. "Tell us what computers were searched."

Agent Salazar recited a long list, which confirmed for Ainsley that Professor Bartow had not been exaggerating: it was virtually every computer she had ever accessed at MIT.

"I want to know more about one computer in particular," said the prosecutor. "The desktop computer in Maclaurin Building four, Room four-three-oh-nine."

Ainsley caught her breath.

"Judge, at this time we'd ask for a stipulation from the

defense that the computer in four-three-oh-nine was the computer used by the defendant for her work with Professor Bartow on a program known as Project Cosmic Company."

"I'm not stipulating to anything," said Connor. "This still feels like an ambush. I have not seen the results of this search, I've had no time to prepare, and—"

"The objection is overruled," the judge said, cutting him off. "The prosecution can link the defendant to the computer through another witness, if necessary. But I'm going to hear this testimony. Proceed, Mr. Goodkin."

Perhaps it was paranoia on Ainsley's part, but something about the judge's demeanor suggested that her good graces toward the defense, so evident when Vlad was on the witness stand, might suddenly be coming to an end.

"Thank you, Your Honor," said Goodkin. "Agent Salazar, I direct your attention to government exhibit twenty-two on the screen. Can you tell me what that is?"

An image flashed on the same projection screen that Connor had used. It was the prosecution's turn for a slide show.

"Yes," said Salazar. "That is a document that was retrieved from the hard drive of the computer in question."

Connor leaned closer to Ainsley and whispered, "What is that?"

"I've never seen it," she answered, but she was studying it quickly. So was Judge Larkin.

"Mr. Goodkin," the judge said, "it's getting late in the day, and we're all tired. Can you give me a quick summary of what we're looking at here?"

"Surely. This is a map of the world."

"I can see *that*," the judge snapped. "I'm talking about these colored dots. One, two, three, four—about a dozen big red dots."

"Each of those red dots denotes a city in which there is a major stock or commodities exchange. "New York, Chicago, London, Tokyo, and so on."

"Got it," the judge said. "What about those blue dots scattered all over the map like a bad case of the measles? I can't even count how many. There must be a thousand of them. What are they?"

Goodkin stepped closer to the screen. "Why don't we let the document speak for itself," he said as he pushed the button on his remote control. An image flashed on the screen. It was typewritten text inside a colored comment bubble. "Agent Salazar, please tell the court what this image is."

"It's a file note that our tech experts found attached to the map in the computer at issue."

"Can you read what it says, please?"

"Yes. It reads as follows. 'Advances in high-frequency financial trading have made light propagation delays between geographically separated exchanges relevant. MAP KEY: Red dots indicate the location of major exchanges worldwide. Blue dots indicate, to a reasonable degree of mathematical certainty, the optimal locations from which to coordinate the statistical arbitrage of pairs of space-like separated securities.'"

"In plain English, what does that mean?"

"This map shows you where to put your computer servers if you want to be the fastest high-frequency trader at the world's biggest exchanges."

Connor looked at Ainsley, who tried to tell him with her eyes that she knew nothing about this map.

Connor rose. "Your Honor, I'd like a moment to confer with my client."

"I'll bet you would."

"Just to be clear, Your Honor, I'm not suggesting that the defense is in any way concerned about this document. Regardless of who made it, what it is, or how it got on this computer in Cambridge, I don't see how it is at all relevant to the charges that my client stole computer code from Hilbert Trading Group in New York."

"Mr. Goodkin, do you care to explain?" the judge asked.

"Surely," said the prosecutor. "As the government will show at trial, the defendant had a two-part scheme. First, she realized that the algorithm she created for Hilbert was worth a lot more than the hundred thousand dollars Hilbert paid her. So she stole it back. Second, she created this map and planned to sell it as a package with her stolen algorithm. That package could launch its new owner to the top of the heap in the new high-frequency trading world that her algorithm created."

"I'm sorry, what did he just say?" asked Connor.

"I'm not sure I follow it, either," the judge said.

"It sounds complicated, Your Honor, but it's a straightforward concept. It's not a perfect analogy, but imagine if you will a brilliant astrophysicist who is clever enough to create an algorithm that shuts down every GPS navigation system in America. Then she's savvy enough to position herself as the only shop in town selling road maps."

"Judge, this is pure fantasy," said Connor. "We have to get back to what is alleged in the indictment. My client is accused of stealing something she created, which makes no sense. She has already demonstrated at the bail hearing that she didn't need to steal back her own algorithm to sell it to anyone. It's in her head. She could have written it down on a stack of cocktail napkins at a bar if she wanted to."

The judge held up her hands to signal *enough*, if not "*I surrender.*" The courtroom was silent.

"It's Friday and I've had a tough week," the judge said. "This lesson in Physics one-oh-one has been fascinating, but frankly, it's triggering a doozy of a migraine. We'll pick this up on Monday morning, at which time Mr. Jameson will have the opportunity to cross-examine Agent Salazar to his metaphysical heart's content. We're adjourned," she said with a crack of the gavel.

"All rise!"

Behind Ainsley it sounded like the clamor of an out-of-step marching band as the press and dozens of spectators rose along with Ainsley and the lawyers. Silence returned just long enough for the judge to reach her chambers. The thud of her door closing was like a starting pistol for courtroom chaos. Reporters rushed to the rail, peppering Ainsley with questions from a distance.

Did you steal the code?

How much have you been offered for that map?

Do you have a Swiss bank account?

Connor took her by the elbow. "Let's see if the bailiff will let us use another exit."

She followed her lawyer away from the rail, away from the mob of reporters that suddenly had "breaking news." The prosecutor approached and stopped Connor before they reached the bailiff. He was speaking to Connor, but Ainsley could overhear.

"Hilbert asked me to launch the nuclear weapons at this

hearing. I didn't. Not even close. It gets much worse for your client."

"I need to know exactly what that search at MIT turned up," said Connor.

"Call me tomorrow. I'll walk you through it this weekend. I may even have a deal for you to take back to your client," he said, glancing at Ainsley. "I'm a very reasonable guy."

He walked away, heading straight toward the rail, seemingly eager to talk to the press.

"Let's get out of here," Connor said to her. "You and I seriously need to talk."

SEVENTEEN

They made a quick and almost clean exit from the courthouse. Ainsley hailed a cab as Connor fended off one pesky reporter who followed them all the way down the granite steps to the curb.

"No, for the tenth time, there is no Swiss bank account," he told the reporter. He slid into the rear seat beside Ainsley and slammed the door shut. The cab pulled away.

"There isn't one, right?" he said. "Please tell me there's no Swiss bank account."

"That's not funny, Connor."

"Sorry."

"It's in the Cayman Islands."

The cab took them straight to Connor's office. His assistant had already left for the day, so it was just the two of them. Connor loosened his tie and was hanging his jacket on the back of the door when Ainsley's cell rang.

She recognized the incoming number and sighed. "I have to take this," she said.

"Go ahead."

"I mean alone."

Connor looked around his tiny office, as if to say *where do you expect me to go?*

"I need a minute," she said.

"I'll check out the hallway," he said, and then he stepped out.

Ainsley braced herself and answered the call. To her relief, it was just a recorded message, not a real person on the line. "*This call is for . . .*" the recording began, then halted for the pseudo-personal intrusion: "*Ainsley Grace—*"

Ainsley hung up. She knew what the call was about, and she'd heard the message too many times before. She opened the door and called Connor in from the hallway.

"Who was it?" he asked.

"Nobody."

He took a seat in his desk chair. "No need to be secretive. It's okay if you're dating someone. We're old friends."

"I spent the last month working eighty hours a week on a high-frequency trading algorithm. Do you really think I'm dating someone?"

"I'm just saying that you don't have to send me out in the hall. If you're seeing someone, I'm happy for you."

"I'm not seeing anyone."

"Then who was on the phone?"

"Nobody."

"Why won't you tell me?"

"Because it literally was *nobody.* It was a recorded message."

"Then why did you have to take the call in private?"

She breathed in and out, not really wanting to get into it. But when Connor got fixated on something, he was like a dog with a bone. It was the lawyer in him.

"It's a collection agency, okay? Sometimes it's a recording, and sometimes there's a real person on the line who I have to beg for more time to pay."

"A collection agency?"

"My grandmother went into a skilled nursing facility before she died. When Medicare ran out, they were ready to kick her out onto the street unless somebody personally guaranteed a private pay arrangement. Gramm raised me after my mother died. I couldn't just let them boot her out the door. I was eighteen, so I signed."

"How much do you owe?"

"About two hundred and sixty-five thousand dollars."

"Fuck! Oh, sorry. I know how you hate pointless f-bombs."

"It's okay. That one wasn't pointless."

"So where do things stand now with the collection agency?"

"I've been negotiating and buying time. But they're about ready to turn it over to the lawyers and sue me, which is the last thing I need now. That's why I had to take the call."

Connor actually groaned.

"Don't worry, counselor. I will figure out some way to pay you. Eventually."

"That's not what I'm groaning about," he said, a hint of anger kicking in. "Why do you keep raising that? Do you think all I care about is getting paid? Fine, I have this shitty little office and a legal assistant who's been on semi–maternity leave for two years because I can only afford to pay her two days a week. Things haven't come easy. But I'm doing okay."

"Sorry, I wasn't suggesting that you're about to close up shop."

"Then stop bringing up the money. Is it really that hard for you to accept somebody doing something nice for you?"

"*Nice*? Is that what you're doing? Being *nice*?"

"Okay, that came out wrong."

"I don't need you or Professor Bartow or anyone else being nice to me. I got plenty of that after my mom died."

"You're missing my point."

"What *is* your point?"

"I care about you. I care about what happens to you."

She looked away, then back, saying nothing.

Connor glanced around his office, his gaze sweeping across one crappy piece of furniture to the next. "And sometimes I just wish I'd stayed in Boston."

Ainsley looked away again. Part of her wanted to say "*me too.*" But life was too complicated already.

"I'm sorry," said Connor. "I shouldn't have said that."

"It's okay," she said, that *me too* still rolling toward the tip of her tongue. But it didn't come. "It's really okay."

Connor sat up straighter in his chair, more businesslike. "The debt doesn't help your defense. If Goodkin finds out about it, he will certainly use it as evidence of your motive to steal and sell the algorithm and the map."

"I know. But like I said before, everybody at Hilbert who knew about that algorithm had serious motive to steal it and sell it."

"Unfortunately, you're the only one who has been charged."

"I think it was Vladimir."

"What about Vladimir?"

"You asked me before who would hire someone to come into the office and steal my computer, and then frame me for stealing trade secrets. I think it was Vladimir. Not once would he even look me in the eye in that courtroom."

"Look, Ainsley. Criminal defense lawyers engage in pop psychology every day, and eye contact is of course part of that unscientific equation. But we need much more than that to convince a judge that Vladimir framed you."

"There's more."

"Let's start with motive," said Connor. "Vladimir paid you to create the algorithm. He owns it. Why would he pay somebody else to steal it and make it look like you did it?"

"That's a tough question. And it's taken me awhile to figure out the answer."

"Oh, you actually have an answer? That's good, because I can't imagine one. Let's hear it."

"I created that algorithm to give Hilbert a competitive advantage. An advantage that in no way violates any laws."

"That's not the issue."

"Yes, it is. Here's my theory: Vladimir intends to use my algorithm in ways that I never intended. In ways that *do* violate the law."

"Fine, let's accept that premise. I still don't see why he would go to the trouble of setting you up as a thief."

"Let me make this as simple as I can. Think of the universe in which all these electronic high-frequency trades take place as a black box. It's technologically feasible to pull algorithms out of the box. That's how people found Carnival and the Boston Shuffler, which you showed the judge in those graphs at the hearing."

"I'm with you so far."

"But it's much more complicated to figure out *who* is using that algorithm. It's not impossible. But it is a lot more difficult."

"Now you're kind of losing me."

"Stay with me," said Ainsley. "Here's the scenario. Vladimir uses my algorithm in a way that breaks the law. Someone looks inside the black box and sees that the algorithm is being used to break the law. Vladimir's response to law enforcement is as follows. That algorithm was stolen by Ainsley. She sold it to somebody. I have no idea who is using that algorithm to break the law. But it sure isn't me."

Connor took a minute, then finally broke the silence. "It adds up. But it's extremely devious."

Ainsley nodded in agreement. "We need to do some digging on Vlad. It wouldn't surprise me at all if 'Devious' turns out to be his middle name."

EIGHTEEN

On Saturday afternoon Ainsley was back in Chinatown. She walked the long way from the Metro station to Columbus Park, steering clear of Peal Street and the surrounding federal complex. She figured it would be worth a few extra steps to avoid even a passing glance at the federal detention center, but there was no tricking herself into not thinking about her night behind bars. The building and memories were right there, whether Ainsley looked or not. She wondered if her cell mate was still locked up.

Watch your backside, pretty girl.

Columbus Park was a small green space directly across the street from the federal courthouse and, more important, the Bangkok Grocery Center. Ainsley decided that she would make a Thai dinner. It was Connor's favorite.

I'm doing something nice. You got a problem with that?

Ainsley stopped at the edge of the park. Chinese opera singers were performing along the walkway. A small audience had gathered in the spotty shade of a tall maple tree that was still working on its new leaves. It was the first legit spring Saturday of the year, and a few sun-starved New Yorkers were pushing it a bit too far. It definitely wasn't bathing suit and tanning weather, at least not by Ainsley's standards.

She watched and listened a few minutes longer. It was a nice diversion. Connor was meeting with Goodkin at the U.S. Attorney's office at that very moment. It was the follow-up to the prosecutor's promise that "things would get worse" for Ainsley—and that he might have a deal to offer.

Her cell rang. She didn't recognize the incoming number, but she answered anyway.

"Is this Ainsley? Ainsley Grace?"

The man sounded Chinese—*Ahnslee*—which was oddly coincidental, given where she was. "Who's asking?"

"I have important information for you."

Ainsley hesitated. This was starting to sound a little James Bond. "Information about what?"

"Mr. Vladimir."

"Vladimir Kosov?"

"Ay, ay, ay," he said, or at least that was what Ainsley heard. For all she knew, he was cursing at her in Cantonese. "No last names," he said. "Meet me outside building at sixty Hudson Street. Come alone."

"I don't even know who you are."

"I one of the blue dots."

More than a little James Bond. A dash of Jason Bourne, too. "Are you saying—"

He hung up before Ainsley could finish her question, but it didn't matter. She knew what he was saying: he was somehow connected to one of the optimal locations on earth for placement of HFT supercomputers.

It was possible that he was just a wiseacre who'd learned about the map with blue dots through the media coverage of yesterday's hearing. But if it was no prank—and if he was, in fact, one of the blue dots—this might be the break she needed. It was worth a three-minute cab ride to find out.

She hailed a taxi and went.

NINETEEN

The taxi dropped Ainsley in front of the old Western Union Building on Hudson Street. She gazed upward, taking in nineteen hues of red brick, darker to lighter, that shaded the multi-tiered building's rise from street to sky.

For decades it was one of the most recognizable buildings in Tribeca, incorporating elements of German Expressionism and Art Deco, its massive footprint occupying an entire city block. After the telegrams stopped in 1973, it became a telecommunications center, eventually transforming into one of the most important internet hubs in the world. Nearly a million square feet of floor space sit above the very hole in the ground from which the fiber-optic cables serving Manhattan sprout. Apart from security guards who shoo away anyone they catch snapping photographs, nary a human being can be found inside the building. This was the land of hollowed-out floors, steel shelves, routers, switches, and servers—a quintessential "carrier hotel."

It was also a hub for high-frequency trading.

Or at least it had been. Ainsley noticed a moving truck parked outside the Hudson Street entrance to the building. Workers were loading computer servers. As Ainsley knew from her experience at Hilbert, high-frequency traders had once flocked to Tribeca to gain the all-important advantage of a millisecond or two over their competitors in the Financial District. But the race was no longer between Wall Street and Hudson Street. The battleground had shifted to places like New Jersey.

And to other blue dots on the map.

Ahnslee?

It was the voice from the phone call. Ainsley turned to see a middle-aged man with dyed black hair who was wearing an even blacker trench coat. "Who are you?"

"Walk with me," he said, as he started up the sidewalk.

Ainsley matched his leisurely stride toward the corner.

"Your map with blue dots could have made me a very rich man," he said.

She saw no point playing dumb. "That map isn't mine."

"Okay. Whatever you say."

"How did you see the map?"

"I have friend very interested in your case."

"Who?"

"Nobody. He like lots of people. Court junkie. This map now public document, all over internet. Last night, my friend, he call me. Friend say, 'Sven'—Sven not my real name. I make that part up, so you don't know who I am."

"Cute, Sven. But ten seconds ago you used a conditional perfect. Knock off the bad English. It's a lame disguise."

"Got me. Friend say: 'Sven, your property is marked with a blue dot on that map in the court case.'"

Ainsley glanced up at the old telecommunications center. "Are you trying to tell me that you own this building?"

"No, no. My warehouse is in Hong Kong. Industrial Estate. Right next to big new data center for Hong Kong Exchange. Blue dot right on it."

"Colocation," said Ainsley. "High-frequency traders want your property to shave milliseconds off their trading time."

"Want it bad. Two firms offer me fifty million dollars."

"So the map did make you a rich man."

"I rich man already. One of first to lease space for servers here at sixty Hudson. I come here when stupid Wall Street bankers still think 'carrier hotel' leave Godiva chocolate on the pillow and give Starwood points. Now we move to New Jersey, I make even more money. But Industrial Estate slipped through my fingers. I should be richer."

"The Hong Kong deal fell through?"

He chuckled, but not because he found any of this funny. "Mr. Tom Smith and his negotiator threaten to give me a new address with permanent view of water at bottom of Junk Bay. I forced to sell warehouse to them at half price."

"Who is this Tom Smith?"

He paused, his expression turning very serious. "My worst nightmare," he said. "Now yours."

TWENTY

Ainsley dialed Connor on her cell. She needed to talk to him. It went to his voice mail.

"Connor, call me."

Her walk and talk with "Sven" had taken her all the way around the telecommunications building. By the time they'd returned to the moving vans that were taking Sven's servers to New Jersey, Ainsley had everything she needed to bust the government's case wide open. Almost.

"I need you to testify for me in court," she'd told Sven.

"No problem."

"You'll do it?"

"Yes. You give me algorithm, I testify for you in court."

"I can't do it."

"Then I get amnesia."

Ainsley definitely should have seen that coming.

She dialed Connor one more time. Voicemail again. He was probably still in his meeting with Goodkin at the justice center. She jumped in a cab and headed for Foley Square. Sven's talk of blue dots and colocation in Hong Kong had triggered a theory, which she could test with a few quick mathematical calculations. She started doing them on her phone in the back seat of the cab, and she continued on the park bench outside the building. Twenty minutes later, she was still so deep in thought that she almost missed Connor as he walked right past her on his way to the Metro.

"Connor!"

She sprang from the bench and caught up with him at the stairwell. He stopped and looked at her, his expression almost apologetic.

"It didn't go well," he said. "Goodkin didn't even offer me a deal. I think he's starting to dig on all the media coverage. He's taking this case to trial."

"I don't care about him," she said, her voice racing with excitement. "I got it: China. That's Vladimir's angle."

"What are you talking about?"

"Remember how I said that Vladimir was going to use my algorithm in a way that I never intended? I figured it out. All the games that high-frequency traders have played in Western markets, Vladimir is going to apply to stock trades in Chinese mainland companies."

"How?"

She spoke quickly, telling him about the phone call from "Sven," the walk around the telecommunications building, and the warehouse in Hong Kong, right next door to the data center.

"We need to get this Sven downtown to talk to the FBI," said Connor.

"That's not going to happen," said Ainsley. "There's a quid

pro quo: his testimony in exchange for my algorithm. Or he gets amnesia."

"Sounds like he's only slightly less slimy than Vladimir," said Connor.

"It's fine. We don't need him. At least I know what Vladimir is up to."

"Maybe you know. But I can't say that I totally understand what you're so excited about."

She took a breath and forced herself to slow down. "Let me start at the beginning. This year, for the first time ever, stock in Chinese mainland companies is being listed on the Hong Kong Exchange. It used to be only on the Shanghai Exchange. Now it's on both. It's called cross-border listing."

"Okay. So?"

"So, just like there are time lags of milliseconds between stock trades of companies like Microsoft or Apple that are listed on more than one exchange in the United States, there will be time lags of milliseconds between stock trades of Chinese mainland companies that are listed on both the Shanghai Exchange and the Hong Kong Exchange. Those time lags are gold to high-frequency traders. It's as if the Great Wall of China has suddenly gone Wall Street."

"And why is Vlad sitting so pretty?"

"The Hong Kong Exchange is well aware of the games that high-frequency traders have been playing. So they created a data center that, in theory, equalizes things and makes it impossible to take advantage of these time lags."

"So, if I'm following you correctly, Vladimir has figured out a way to override that equalization."

"That's where my time-synchronization algorithm comes in.

He owns the warehouse right next door to the Hong Kong data center. Launching my program from that location could throw off every other trader with a server in that data center by a millisecond or two, and no one would know it. Vladimir would have the millisecond advantage he needs over everyone else who trades Chinese mainland stocks that are listed on both the Shanghai and Hong Kong Exchanges."

Ainsley could almost see the light bulb switching on over Connor's head. "He's putting himself in the catbird seat to front run Chinese stocks. Is that what you're saying?"

"You got it," said Ainsley. "And if the authorities figure out that my algorithm is being used to undermine the Hong Kong exchange, I'm his scapegoat. He'll say I stole the algorithm and before I went to prison I sold it to the Mafia, the Russian mob, Chinese terrorists—"

"Or worse, Wall Street bankers."

"There you go. Vladimir can blame anybody he wants."

"Now we have a workable defense," said Connor. "But without Sven, how do we prove it? We really do need him to testify."

"No, we don't," said Ainsley, reaching for her phone—her latest calculations. "I'm already on it."

TWENTY-ONE

Ainsley was in her kitchenette making steamed chicken and vegetable dumplings. The wonton wraps were rolled, the filling was mixed, and the pot of water was boiling on the stove. Some might say dumplings are strictly Chinese, but her spices were straight from Bangkok, and lining her bamboo steamer with banana leaves at least made her feel like she was cooking Thai style. Except that she'd forgotten to buy banana leaves.

"Connor? I found something you can do."

He was out hunting for banana leaves when her cell phone rang. It was Professor Bartow. She nearly dropped the phone into the boiling water.

"I read about yesterday's hearing," he said. "I want to help."

"Thank you. I appreciate that."

"I don't mean that in a general way. I mean, I have a specific idea of *how* I can help."

She wiped the fish sauce from her hands and stepped away from the hot stove. "Okay. I'm listening."

•••••

Connor hurried up the subway steps and continued down the sidewalk with Ainsley's banana leaves and bottle of white wine in a brown paper bag. The entire trip would have taken less than thirty minutes if he'd gone straight to the Bangkok Grocery Center, which was where Ainsley had told him to go. Out of curiosity—just to see if Ainsley was wrong—he'd stopped at two other specialty grocers along the way and checked for banana leaves. They didn't carry them. In fact, both grocers had told him to "Try the Bangkok Grocery Center." Ainsley had been right, of course. She usually was. Darn near *always* was.

Funny thing: Connor kind of liked it that way.

"Got a cigarette, buddy?" asked an old homeless man. He was sitting cross-legged on the sidewalk, he and his puppy wrapped in a ratty plaid blanket. Connor was tempted to roll him a banana leaf. Instead, he gave him a buck and crossed the street with the green light.

He'd made a deal with Ainsley not to talk about her case tonight, but it was hard to shut off his mind. His Saturday morning meeting with the prosecutor had not gone well. The government was prepared, if not eager, to take her case to trial. If Ainsley was going to prove that she was framed, they needed Sven to testify about his dealings with Vladimir and Hilbert Trading. The calculations that Ainsley had worked out in Foley Square, while Connor was at his meeting, would prove that Vlad was planning to game the Hong Kong Exchange—she was convinced of it. To an astrophysicist, there was no greater certainty than mathematical certainty. Truth be told, however, not even Connor understood her equations, not even after she'd explained them to him three times. To a judge and jury, Ainsley's "evidence" would be just numbers—a confusing, unconvincing string of numbers.

Darn near always right. This time, however, Ainsley was wrong.

The elevator was still broken, so Connor hoofed it up four floors to Ainsley's apartment, his footfalls echoing through the old stairwell. He'd taken her extra key with him, but he knocked anyway before letting himself in.

"Banana leaf boy," he announced as he closed the door behind him. Enticing smells of spicy chicken wafted across the apartment, but the kitchen was empty.

"In here," Ainsley called from the bedroom.

He removed the bottle of wine from the paper bag, smiled mischievously, and wondered how Ainsley would look wearing only a banana leaf. Then he came to his senses.

Not gonna happen.

Ainsley was stuffing a change of clothes into an overnight bag when he stopped in the doorway. "Where are you going?"

"Taiwan," she said, pulling on her coat.

Connor's jaw nearly dropped. The mysterious plane ticket to Taiwan had been problem number one in Ainsley's assortment of legal troubles.

"I'm kidding," she said. "I'm sorry about dinner. I just got off the phone with Professor Bartow. I have to go to Cambridge."

"Now?"

"Yes. If I hurry, I can catch the next train."

"What do you have to go to Cambridge for?"

She went to him and stood close, her bag over her shoulder. Then she kissed him—just a peck, but it was on lips.

"Answers," she said.

TWENTY-TWO

Ainsley's train rolled into Boston around nine o'clock Saturday evening. It was just a cab ride across the river to Cambridge.

The plan was to meet at Professor Bartow's office. She didn't go straight there. It was a slight diversion, but there was an important stop she needed to make.

Ainsley climbed the creaky wood stairs, crossed the covered porch, and knocked on the front door of the old frame house on Vassar Street. An old man came to the door and opened it. In the dim yellow glow of the porch light he looked at her quizzically for a moment, and then smiled with recognition.

"Well if it isn't the one and only Ainsley Grace. What a nice surprise."

"Great to see you, too. Am I interrupting anything?"

"No, no. Come in, please."

"Thank you, Dean."

Dean Thomas Bales was retired, but everyone still called him "Dean." Ainsley's mother had called him "Tommy Gun," for the way he would critique her work with a spray of ideas in machine-gun fashion, leaving her theories riddled with holes. The idea for the worldwide telescope had been his, but the entire physics department benefited from Dean Bales' groundwork and vision. Professor Bartow found the money and brainpower to implement it.

"I was just going to pour myself a cup of tea," he said. "Would you care to join me, Ainsley?"

"I'd like that very much. Thank you."

She followed him down the hall to the kitchen. They talked broadly about her research, neither one mentioning the indictment or upcoming trial. The elephant in the room quickly revealed itself.

"I need your advice," she said as he poured from the teapot. "Somehow, I have to convince the department to lift my suspension from Project Cosmic Company."

"I wish a retired old dean could be of help."

"You still have an office in Maclaurin four."

"Yes, I still have an office. I don't get there very often these days. Not with this arthritis."

Ainsley squeezed a wedge of lemon into her tea. "And you still sit ex-officio on the departmental governance committee."

"I do."

Ainsley hesitated. Then she went for it. "Were you at the meeting where the vote was taken on my suspension?"

The dean walked slowly back to the stove and turned off the gas. The flames sputtered and then went out. "Ainsley, you know I can't talk about votes at department meetings."

She nodded. "I know."

He returned to the kitchen table and took a seat across from her.

"I notice you're not wearing one of your signature Hawaiian shirts," said Ainsley.

He smiled, but it was a sad one. "It's my form of protest."

"Against my suspension?"

"Well, I told you I can't talk to you about department meeting votes. But okay, yes: I'm protesting your suspension. No more Hawaiian shirts."

"Funny. Professor Bartow is doing the same thing."

"Is that so?"

"Yes. It's kind of an interesting pattern, isn't it?"

"What do you mean?"

"He followed in your footsteps on the global telescope. He picked up your tradition of wearing Hawaiian shirts. Now he even follows your lead on the protest. I guess imitation is the highest form of flattery."

"You might say that."

Ainsley wrapped her hands around her steaming teacup, feeling the warmth. "Can I ask you a question?"

"Sure."

"For years people have told me how closely you worked with my mother and Professor Bartow. But I honestly don't know that much about the actual work dynamic."

"What do you want to know?"

"Well, for example, take Professor Bartow's pattern of conduct that I mentioned. Is that the way your team operated: dress alike, act alike, the two protégés a reflection of their mentor?"

"Your mother? A reflection?" He flashed a nostalgic smile.

"No way. She was like you. We were butting heads all the time."

"I suppose that can be a good thing."

"A good thing? Are you kidding me? It's a *great* thing. That kind of give-and-take inspires big ideas, like that whitepaper you wrote for the journal on time synchronization. That was a huge breakthrough for the telescope."

"Thank you."

"It was a *real* original thought."

She almost blushed. "It just kind of came to me."

"Just like your mother," he said, and then his warm smile faded.

Ainsley took notice. "Is something wrong?"

He looked away, and then drew a breath. His hand trembled slightly as he laid his spoon aside. "Let me tell you something about Professor Bartow and original thought," he said.

Ainsley waited.

Finally, the dean drew another breath and blinked slowly, as if it pained him to utter an unkind word about anyone. "Or should I say the lack of it."

TWENTY-THREE

It was late, but Ainsley called ahead, and Professor Bartow told her that it wasn't too late. They met on campus in his office at the Maclaurin building. It was about videotape from MIT security cameras.

"The FBI never told me what they were looking for or what they found when they came here with a warrant to search our computers," he said. "I was absolutely stunned when I read about the high-frequency trading map that the prosecutor introduced into evidence at yesterday's court hearing."

"Ditto," said Ainsley. "Especially when he said it came from the computer that I used for Project Cosmic Company."

"So you didn't put it there?"

It was the most pointed question he'd asked since her indictment, and it took her aback. "No. I didn't put it there. Until yesterday, I'd never heard of a map like that one."

"Me neither. That's why I told you to come. Because if you didn't put it there, and I didn't put it there, then we need to find out who did."

He switched on his computer, and they were soon bathed in the green glow of the LCD monitor. "This could take a while."

"What could?"

"I checked with our security department. We keep closed-circuit video from our security cameras for ninety days. Every person who went in or out of that computer room in the last ninety days should be on that video. And it's all here on my computer."

"Does the FBI know you have this?"

"Of course. They already have their copy. But between the two of us, we should be able to spot anyone in that room who doesn't belong there."

"Okay, let's do it."

"Could be a long night. You want some coffee?"

"No, thanks. I just finished a pot of tea with Dean Bales."

He shot a reproving look. "No offense, Ainsley, but it's after eleven, I've been sitting here in my office waiting for you, and you stopped to have tea with Dean Bales?"

"Sorry. I know that seems rude. But it was extremely important that I talk to him."

"More important than this?"

"Much more," said Ainsley. "See, the minute I saw that high-frequency trading map in the courtroom, I was reminded of the map right there on your wall. The Project Cosmic Company map."

"Maps of the world do tend to look alike. What's your point?"

"I started looking more closely at the location of the blue dots. Granted, there are hundreds of them on the high-frequency trading map. But you know what? It turns out that every server location for Project Cosmic Company is also a blue dot on the HFT map."

"Interesting coincidence."

"Yeah. It is. You know what else is strange?"

"What?"

"You never told me how much you disliked my mother."

"Whoa, that's a pretty abrupt segue. Where did that come from?"

"The smartest person I've ever met. And quite possibly, the most genuine."

He scoffed nervously, but he seemed to understand that Ainsley was referring to the dean. "First of all, I didn't dislike your mother. For Pete's sake, the whitepaper we were writing was published after she died. I put her name as lead author."

"Dean Bales told me that you wanted her name removed from it. He insisted that it stay on and that her name be first because it was mostly her work."

"Well, all I can say about that is poor Dean Bales must be getting awfully senile in his old age."

Ainsley's glare tightened. "Do you know when my passkey at Hilbert Trading Group disappeared?

"What is it with all these questions?"

"The prosecutor's theory is that I gave my passkey to an accomplice, who then reactivated it to enter the building after hours and steal my computer with my algorithm on it."

"I'm well aware of the charges against you, Ainsley."

"I think you're also well aware of the truth: I didn't give my passkey to anyone."

He shifted uncomfortably in his chair.

"I told the FBI that I must have lost it," she said. "But

that's not true, either, is it? You know when I 'lost' it," she said, making air quotes. "Two weeks ago, when I came to Cambridge to work on Project Cosmic Company."

"Well, then, all the more reason for us to review these security tapes. They might show us who took your passkey."

"It won't be on those tapes."

"How do you know before we've even looked?"

"I kept my purse in your office."

Professor Bartow suddenly looked numb. "That doesn't mean—"

"I know *exactly* what it means," said Ainsley.

He settled back into his chair, his gaze fixed on the map that covered his wall. He seemed ready to say something. Ainsley gave him a nudge.

"Tell me what you did, Professor."

He didn't respond right away. Finally, he spoke.

"It was like déjà vu," he said in a distant voice. "Your mother and I were a couple of bright doctoral candidates, working side by side. Dean Bales selected us to his dream team, and we were going to build a global telescope to search for earthlike planets orbiting other stars. It didn't take long for your mother to outshine everybody on the team, to become the clear front-runner to lead the project. Then she got sick. It wasn't the way I wanted to earn the nod to lead this project, but I took it. I ran with it. I did one hell of an amazing job. It took eighteen years, but finally this thing is working. It's taking off. And then you walked in the door."

"You invited me."

"I didn't *invite* you. My signature was on the letter from the department, but Dean Bales invited you. I suppose I could have found a reason to ding you. Instead, I took a long look in the mirror and said 'Fine. Don't be petty, Howard. She's a kid. Are you really afraid that she's going to outshine *you*?'"

Ainsley said nothing. She just watched as he shook his head and released a mirthless chuckle. "And so what does *the kid* do? She publishes the most amazing whitepaper of the twenty-first century on time-synchronization algorithms."

"It's not the most a—"

"Oh, shut up! Yes, it is."

Ainsley sat in silence.

The professor's angry smile tightened. "And then," he said, chuckling again. "And *then* Wall Street comes knocking. You receive this incredible six-figure offer for three or four weeks of consulting work at Hilbert, and you ask for my advice. *My* advice. 'Go!' I say. *Go,go, go.* You go, get rich, waste that beautiful brain, and become one more physicist who sells out to Wall Street, and please don't ever come back."

Ainsley felt her anger rising. Professor Bartow had seemed so genuine at the time, and his words of encouragement had been the tipping point in her decision to work at Hilbert.

"Then one night," he said, "I'm sitting here in my office staring at my map on the wall, and I get this flash of inspiration. I think to myself: Maybe Ainsley's onto something. If everybody on my team took just three weeks a year to dazzle these Wall Street firms, we could fund Project Cosmic Company without ever having to beg for money again."

He stopped, but Ainsley wasn't going to let it end there.

"You created that map," she said. "Didn't you?"

"Yeah," he said. "It's mine. I took it to Hilbert Trading Group and to Mr. Kosov himself. You know what he did?"

Ainsley shook her head.

"He laughed at me."

"He laughed?"

"Yeah. Have you checked the GPS coordinates of those dots?"

She had, but she wasn't going to bring up Sven's warehouse in Hong Kong. "Not all of them."

"Most are in densely populated urban hubs, where the server locations are already spoken for. The rest are out in the middle of the ocean or in the Arctic Circle, or some other place that you can't feasibly operate from. It's a worthless piece of academic shit. That's what he told me."

Ainsley didn't bother to tell him that Vladimir had actually put it to use in Hong Kong. "I'm sorry."

"Don't patronize me. It's bad enough as it is. When Kosov laughed—and I mean he literally laughed—something came over me. Wall Street was willing to pay *you* the equivalent of over a million dollars a year. But they laugh at me."

"That's not my fault."

"No, it's not. But I needed to know what the hell you were doing. I needed to *see it*," he said, his voice hissing. "I needed to wrap my mind around whatever it was that was so fucking special."

"So you stole my passkey."

"Yeah. When you came up for the weekend. It was attached to your key chain."

"And you went into my office at Hilbert and stole my computer."

"No. That's where I screwed up. I should have done it myself. I hired somebody to do it."

There was a noise outside the office, the sound of approaching footfalls, and they made Ainsley start.

"Relax," he said. "It's just the FBI."

"I didn't call the FBI."

"I did," he said as he opened his shirt. He was wearing a wire. "The guy I hired to steal your computer turned me in this morning. I told them it was all your idea. The FBI offered me no jail time if I wore a wire and proved it."

Ainsley glared in disbelief. "You're pathetic."

He sighed with resignation. "Not so pathetic that I could actually go through with it. Agent Salazar heard everything I just said. You're free, Ainsley Grace. Congratulations. You and your mother win again."

The door opened. Agent Salazar and two other agents entered the office. Ainsley and the professor rose.

"Stay where you are!" Salazar shouted. Two agents blocked the doorway. Salazar hurried past Ainsley and went to Professor Bartow. He offered no resistance as the agent cuffed his wrists behind his back, read him his Miranda rights, and placed him under arrest. Salazar directed him toward the door, then stopped briefly on their way out.

"You're one lucky woman," said Salazar.

Ainsley didn't answer. Professor Bartow had one more thing to say.

"I just needed to know what was on your computer," he said. "I never dreamed that you would be charged with stealing your own algorithm. I never wanted you to go to jail. I hope you believe that."

Ainsley's glare only tightened. "I might have bought that line, Howard. Except it's clear to me now that the 'nuclear weapon' the prosecutor threatened to launch after Friday's hearing was *you*. Even before your accomplice turned you in, before the FBI corralled you into wearing a wire, you were planning to lie your way out of this and testify against me at trial, weren't you?"

He didn't deny it.

Ainsley glanced at Salazar, then back at the professor. "You want to know the name my cellmate gave me that night I spent downtown in the detention center? 'Pretty girl.' This scary voice from the top bunk in a pitch-dark jail cell called me 'pretty girl.' I say this with all my heart, Professor: I hope you are just as lucky."

He lowered his head, refusing to look her in the eye. Ainsley watched as the FBI took him away.

EPILOGUE

FOUR MONTHS LATER

Ainsley had her eye on the swan. She was gazing up into the night sky, pointing. "Do you see the long neck and widespread wings?" she asked. "That's the constellation Cygnus."

Connor was at her side. It was 2:00 a.m., and they were sitting on the hood of his car at the end of a lonely gravel road in central Massachusetts, an hour's drive from Cambridge and the city lights of Boston. Coldplay set the mood via CD from the car stereo: *A Sky Full of Stars*, of course.

"I think I see it. But it doesn't look like much of a swan to me."

"That's okay. The star I'm most excited about isn't visible with the naked eye anyway."

"Does it have a name?"

"Kepler twenty-two. It's a yellow dwarf, like our sun, only a little cooler."

Connor glanced at her, then back at the twinkling sky. "There must be billions of yellow dwarfs out there. What's so interesting about this one?"

"Really good question, Connor."

"Hey, I'm a lawyer. It's what I do."

She smiled and pulled her thighs to her chest, her chin above her knees. "Well, here's what's special about Kepler twenty-two. We know it has a planetary system. One of those planets is a little more than twice the size of earth and just the right distance from Kepler twenty-two for liquid water to exist. It's the one star we have found in this vast ocean of stars where there could be a planet like ours."

"How far away is it from us?"

"Six hundred light years."

Connor was admiring her profile in the starlight. "That's really beautiful."

She was still gazing at the heavens. "Yeah. It is."

Project Cosmic Company was going stronger than ever. After Professor Bartow's arrest, Dean Bales came out of retirement to resume leadership over his project. Bartow's criminal trial was set for November, and the expectation was that he would spend the foreseeable future in the male wing of Ainsley's least favorite place, the Metropolitan Correction Center. Ainsley had spent the previous three months at her new *favorite* place on earth. Dean Bales made her the regional head of the observatory in Hawaii that was being linked to the project's worldwide telescope.

She and Connor had stayed in touch by e-mail and Skype. This was her first trip back to the Northeast since the dismissal of all criminal charges against her. It had been Connor's idea that they drive out to the country for an intergalactic tour of her work.

"You ever hear anything from Sven?" asked Connor.

Mere mention of the pseudo-Swede with the Chinese accent made her laugh. "No. Nothing."

"So Vlad got to keep the warehouse that his thug forced Sven to sell him?"

"Yup. Vlad is still there, and Hilbert is the fastest high-frequency trader on the Hong Kong Exchange."

"That sucks. Somebody needs to give ol' Vlad what he's got coming to him."

"Sven is no saint, either."

"I don't mean for Sven's sake. Vlad is almost as bad as Professor Bartow. Bartow was behind the theft of your office computer. But I think Vladimir planted that laptop computer in your apartment that turned up in the FBI's search. He bought that plane ticket to Taiwan in your name to make it look like you were fleeing the country. He knew he was going to misuse your trading algorithm in Hong Kong, and putting you in jail was the best way to keep you under his thumb."

"I agree."

"I wish there was something we could do about that."

"Wish upon a star," she said. "It may come true."

Connor seemed to take her meaning. "Uh-oh."

"Uh-oh what?"

"It may be dark, but I still detect a bit of a cat-that-ate-the-canary expression on your face. Have you been up to no good?"

"Depends on what you mean by 'no good.'"

"A couple weeks ago, I took a closer look at Professor Bartow's trading map," he said.

"What did you see?"

"A lot of blue dots marking the best places on the planet to post a server for high-frequency trading. But what really caught my eye is that one of those blue dots is right on the Big Island in Hawaii."

"Interesting."

"And then I checked the GPS coordinates for the dot, and it is almost exactly where you volunteered to go when Dean Bales took over Project Cosmic Company."

"How 'bout that."

"Yeah, how 'bout that. Of all the locations you could have asked Dean Bales to send you, you pushed for Hawaii—right on a blue dot."

"Amazing."

"Yes. And you know what's even more amazing? I won't pretend to totally understand this. But from what I can gather from the footnotes to the map, the Hawaii location is one of two places on earth that are ideal for high-frequency trading in the Hong Kong market."

"You don't say?"

"Actually, I do say."

Silence fell between them. Then Connor picked up where he'd left off. "So Vlad is playing games in Hong Kong. You're sitting in a roomful of supercomputers in Hawaii, the ideal location to beat any high-frequency trader operating in the Hong Kong Market. What do you do about that?"

"What do you mean?"

"Oh, come on, Ainsley. In your darkest dreams you must have thought about how to bring Vladimir to his knees."

"You mean hypothetically?"

"Sure. Let's talk hypothetically."

Ainsley laughed, then turned serious. "I'd write a monster algorithm to beat the penny jumper at his own game."

"I like it," said Connor. "Hypothetically, I mean."

Ainsley raised her eyes toward the night sky, fixing on the swan. "Six hundred years," she said.

"Six hundred years until what?"

"Until whoever is on that planet orbiting Kepler twenty-two gazes back toward earth and sees the lights go out on Hilbert Trading Group."

He reached over and held her hand. "You are one clever girl, Ainsley Grace."

"Call me Penny," she said. "Penny Jumper."

GREEN-EYED LADY

A SHORT STORY

FEATURING

FBI AGENT ANDIE HENNING

JAMES GRIPPANDO

Outside her bedroom window, the blanket of fallen leaves moved—one footstep at a time.

Andie Henning lay quietly in her bed, her sleeping fiancé at her side. It was a brisk winter night, downright cold by Miami standards. In a city where forty degrees was considered frigid, no more than once or twice a year could Andie light the fireplace and snuggle up to Jack beneath a fluffy down comforter. She slid closer to his body, drawn by his warmth. A gusty north wind rattled the window. The whistle became a howl, but the steady crunching of leaves was still discernible, the unmistakable sound of an approaching stranger.

Flashing images in her head offered a clear view of the lawn, the patio, and the huge almond leaves scattered all about. She could see the path the man had cut, and it led straight to her window.

It had been almost four years since the funeral, and Andie knew the man responsible for her sister's death was in prison. But on nights like these, she would have sworn he was back, in the flesh. The disturbing details of their final confrontation were forever burned into her memory. Most unforgettable of all were those empty, shark-like eyes—eyes so cold and angry that she'd seen her own reflection in the shiny black iris. His eyes still haunted her, as if mocking her pleas to save her sister's life.

His name was Wicassa.

Outside, the wind and leaves were momentarily silent. The digital alarm clock on the nightstand blinked on and off, the way it always did when storms interrupted power. It was stuck on midnight, bathing her pillow with faint pulses of green light.

Green. The color of her eyes. Those amazing green eyes that, with the raven-black hair and high cheekbones of a Native American, made for one exotic beauty.

Andie was in her tenth year with the FBI, the first six in Seattle and the balance in the Miami field office. Hardly a lifelong dream of hers, the bureau had been more of a safe landing for a self-assured thrill seeker. At the training academy, she became only the twentieth woman in bureau history to make the Possible Club, a ninety-eight-percent-male honorary fraternity for agents who shoot perfect scores on one of the toughest firearms courses in law enforcement. Her supervisor in Seattle saw her potential, and she didn't disappoint him—at least not until personal reasons prompted her to put in for a transfer to Miami, about as far away from Seattle as she could get.

Andie heard a knock at the back door. On impulse, she rose and sat at the edge of the bed.

Don't go, she told herself, but it was as if she were being summoned.

Another knock followed, exactly like the first one. On the other side of the king-sized bed, Jack was sleeping soundly. She didn't even consider waking him.

I'll get it.

Andie saw herself rise from the mattress and plant her bare feet on the wood floor. Each step felt colder as she continued down the hall and through the kitchen. The house was completely dark, and she relied more on instinct than sight to maneuver her way to the back door. As she peered out the little beveled window, a gust of wind ripped through the big almond tree, tearing the brownest leaves from the branches. A few were caught in an upward draft and rose into the night, just beyond the faint glow of the porch light. Andie lost sight of them, except for one that seemed to hover above the patio. Another blast of wind sent it soaring upward. Then it suddenly changed direction, came straight toward her, and slammed against the door.

The noise startled her, the door swung open, and a burst of cold air hit her like an Arctic front. Goose bumps covered her arms and legs. Her silk nightgown shifted in the breeze. She somehow knew that she was colder than ever before in her life, but numbness had washed over her. Instinct told her to run, but her feet wouldn't move, defying her fear of the silhouette in the doorway—and of those eyes, those shark-like eyes.

"*Hi, sweetheart,*" the voice came.

"Don't call me sweetheart."

"Is that any way to talk to your daddy?"

"You're not my father."

"You'll never be safe."

With a shrill scream Andie sat bolt upright in bed. A hand brushed her skin, and she screamed again.

"It's okay," said Jack. He moved closer and tried putting his arms around her.

"No!" she said, pushing him away.

"It's okay, it's me."

Her heart was pounding, and she was on the verge of hyperventilation.

"Take a deep breath," said Jack. "Slowly, in and out."

She inhaled, then exhaled, repeating the exercise several times. In a minute or so, the panic subsided. Jack's touch felt soothing now, and she nestled into his embrace.

"Was it that dream again? The one about your . . ." Jack stopped, not sure what to call that man.

"Yes," said Andie. She was staring into the darkness, not even aware that Jack was gently brushing her hair out of her face. "Why am I still having these dreams?"

"It's okay," said Jack. "There's nothing to be afraid of. Try to get some sleep."

She met his kiss and then let him go, stroking his forehead as he drifted off to sleep. He was breathing audibly in the darkness, but she still felt utterly alone. She lay with eyes wide open, listening and praying that there would be no more dreams of knocking at the back door. It wasn't helpful to think about the past, but she couldn't help herself. That was the problem with keeping secrets; you couldn't keep them from yourself.

Andie had never planned on leaving Seattle. Somehow, deep inside, however, she had known from the very beginning that if she visited that man in prison—the man who had let her sister die—she would end up running away from the city, the job, and the people she loved. She would have to find someplace new. She'd gone to see him anyway. It was that important.

And it had been worse than she'd expected. Far worse.

WASHINGTON STATE PENITENTIARY was no place for the superstitious. The address alone was a dark omen: 1313 North 13th Street. The only way to feel worse was to arrive on Friday the thirteenth.

Andie arrived on a Saturday during regular visitation hours. This was personal, not FBI business, and she pulled no favors or special treatment through the warden or the bureau of prisons. In fact, she preferred not to call attention to herself. She'd jumped through the same hoops as anyone else who was not on an inmate's approved list of regular visitors. It had taken two weeks to obtain clearance, plenty of time for her to reconsider her decision. At several points along the five-hour drive from Seattle, she was again tempted to turn back. But she was determined to see this through.

The penitentiary was on 540 acres of farmland in southeast Washington, a veritable fortress in an otherwise scenic valley framed by the Blue Mountains. The town of Walla Walla (the name was from a Native American word meaning "many waters") could only be described as charming, and under different circumstances, Andie might have been tempted to visit one of forty nearby wineries. On this trip, however, her only destination was the state's largest correctional facility, which housed over two-thousand offenders. There were four separate facilities within the institution, each equipped to handle different levels of custody. Andie went to the main institution, a closed custody building that was second only to death row in terms of security.

"This way, please," said the corrections officer at the entrance to Building One.

Upon entering, Andie didn't flash her badge or do anything else to distinguish herself from other visitors. She simply presented herself at the check-in station in accordance with the visitation policy. A female corrections officer conducted a quick inspection to make sure she met the dress code. No transparent or translucent clothing. No bare chest or midriff. Blue jeans were fine, so long as the waistline was not more than three inches below the navel. And, of course, undergarments were mandatory.

"You're clear," said the guard.

Most of the visitors broke off toward the activity center, where inmates in the general population were allowed face-to-face visitation. Andie, however, was routed in another direction.

"Inmate Wicassa has been reassigned to Segregation Unit One," said the guard. "Personal contact visits have been denied."

Only after a moment did it register that Andie was there to see a man named Wicassa. "You mean I drove all the way from Seattle for nothing?" she said.

"He can still have visitors, just no personal contact. You'll be separated by a glass partition."

Andie tried not to show how little she cared. It wasn't as if she'd planned a big hug and kiss for him. "That's fine," she said.

The corrections officer led her down the hall to the visitation area. Another guard showed her to station number three, one of five stations on the visitors' side of the glass partition. The other side was for prisoners, a narrow room about six-feet deep and twenty-feet long with a solid metal door in the rear. Down to Andie's right, a woman was staring at an older inmate through the glass, neither of them saying a word, as if they'd run out of things to talk about after so many years on the opposite sides of prison walls. Andie looked away, not wanting to be caught staring at another's misfortune. She scooted her chair toward the glass, closer to the phone box on the counter.

A buzzer sounded, which gave her a start. On the other side of the glass, the metal door slid open. A gray-haired man dressed in an orange prison jumpsuit entered the room. The door closed behind him. He walked slowly toward the glass and sat in the chair facing Andie. For a moment, they just studied each another from opposite sides of the partitionglass. The name on his breast pocket—WICASSA—was stenciled in black letters, and it was the only way for Andie to know that she'd found the right man. He was a total stranger, except for the way in which he had so profoundly impacted her life.

Three feet away, was all she could think. She was sitting three feet away from the man who had killed her mother.

He was by no means fat, but he was a large man, and Andie surmised that he'd spent countless hours in the prison gym as a younger inmate. The muscles had softened with age, but his expression had hardened into a perpetual scowl. His skin, though brown, had an unhealthy ashen quality that was the prison pallor. It was surprisingly smooth, however, with relatively few wrinkles for his age. A man sentenced to life without parole apparently didn't spend much time worrying about his release. What captivated her most, however, were his black, piercing eyes. They seemed to smolder with anger as he locked like radar onto Andie's pools of green. She could almost feel the hatred coming through the glass.

He pressed the phone to his ear. Andie picked up on her side. Again, there was silence, as if neither one knew where to start. Finally he said, "Those eyes don't lie."

Andie didn't disagree.

He breathed into the phone, something between a scoff and a grunt. "After all these years. You finally want to know about the man who was married to your mother."

Truthfully, she couldn't have cared less about him, but she opted for a more conciliatory response. "I'm actually more interested in my biological father."

"What about him?" Even now, there was bitterness in his voice.

"Whatever you can tell me."

"Why do you want to know?"

"I need to find him, but I don't even know his name."

"And you think I can help you?"

"I hope so. No one I've talked to knows anything about him. You're my last shot."

He flashed a thin smile of disgust. "What are you looking for, a nice little Anglo family reunion? You think they want to make you a part of their family, the little multiethnic bastard that came along when Johnny Green Eyes knocked up some Yakama bitch."

Andie took a breath, refusing to let him get under

her skin. "I want information, that's all. Do you know his name?"

"Of course I know his name. Your mother thought she was so clever, sneaking off the way she did. This went on for months. I knew what was going on, and I told her I wasn't gonna put up with it. For a while there, I believed her when she said it was over. Then you popped out, and . . ."

She looked away, as if to hide those green eyes. Less than two percent of newborns came into the world with eyes of green, and virtually no pureblood Native Americans were born with blue or green. "And you lost control," she said.

"I gave her what she deserved."

Andie could have argued about the punishment fitting the crime, but she wasn't there to defend an adulteress. "So you can help me? You can tell me his name?"

"I could. But why should I?"

"Because it's not my fault that my mother cheated on you. This is important. I wouldn't come here if it weren't really important."

He fell silent again, but Andie could almost see the wheels turning in his head. "All right," he said. "I can give you his name."

"Thank you." Andie pulled a pen and a notepad from her purse. "What is it?"

"Not so fast." He leaned closer to the glass, as if sharing a secret. "First, I need to know what it's worth to you."

"You want me to pay you?"

"I have something you want. All I'm saying is that it's negotiable."

Andie wasn't surprised, but she wasn't pleased, either.

"What do you have in mind?"

"Do you know how long I've been in here?"

"Yes." She'd done her homework. He'd committed his first felony, aggravated assault, long before Andie's birth. After shooting Andie's mother, he copped a plea and served twelve years for second-degree murder. He kept out of trouble—or at least he didn't get caught—for nearly a decade after his release. Then he was convicted of armed robbery, his third violent felony, resulting in a life sentence under Washington's three-strike law.

"Twenty-one of the last thirty-three years," he said. "This is where I been."

It hardly seemed helpful to point out that it was his own damn fault. "That has to be tough," she said.

"Yeah," he said with a mirthless chuckle, "it's tough all right. So here's what we're gonna do. You come back in two weeks. By that time, I should be out of segregation, and I'll have my full visitation rights."

"I can't wait two weeks."

"You're gonna have to. Because I can't get what I want so long as we're sitting on opposite sides of a glass wall."

Andie hesitated, then said, "I'm not smuggling anything in here, if that's what you're suggesting."

"You don't have to bring me nothing. Just show up."

Suddenly, the idea of smuggling contraband didn't sound so bad. "What are you asking me to do?"

His eyes narrowed. "I'm not asking for nothing that doesn't happen here every Saturday morning during general visitation hours."

"Forget it."

"You want to know your father's name or don't you?"

"Name another price."

"There is no other price."

"Then there's no deal."

He shrugged and said, "You'll come around. I can wait. I got nothing but time on my hands."

"I'm not coming back."

"Sure you will. If you're anything like your mother, you'll be back."

"You're repulsive."

"So shoot me. It's not like you and I are blood."

"I'm not doing you any sexual favors."

"Aw, come on, girl. Be reasonable."

She was about to hang up, but he caught her just in time. "George," he said.

Andie looked at him quizzically through the glass.

"Your father's first name is George," he said. "If you want to know the last name, be back in two weeks. Come back with a smile and I'll even wear a condom."

He seemed pleased with himself, but there was nothing Andie could do. He hung up the phone and signaled for the guard. The buzzer sounded. The door opened. Andie watched in silence as the key to her past disappeared behind prison walls.

THE DRIVE BACK TO SEATTLE gave her plenty of time to think. Too much time.

That pathetic excuse for a human being was the only living person who could help her find her biological father. In her entire life, Andie had never even considered searching out her genealogical roots. Suddenly, however, finding some guy named "George" was a matter of life and death. The oncologist confirmed that much when she got back to the hospital on that cloudy, gray morning in Seattle.

"How bad is it?" Andie asked. She'd been waiting for almost an hour to speak with her sister's treating physician at the University of Washington Medical Center, and she ambushed him as soon as he stepped out of the elevator.

"It's an uphill battle," he said.

"What does that mean exactly?"

His deep sigh almost made an answer unnecessary. "Your sister is a fighter, but we can't give her the level of chemotherapy she needs without a successful bone marrow transplant."

Andie tried to keep her composure, but after all the sleepless nights and unanswered prayers, fear and frustration were taking control. "I don't understand. We're twins. Why didn't her body accept my bone marrow?"

"Because you're not identical twins. That puts you in the same category as any other sibling, which means that this was an allogeneic transplant, not syngeneic. The chances of an HLA match between siblings is only about thirty- to forty-percent."

"Okay, so I'm not a match. What about unrelated donors? Can we try that route?"

"I'm afraid the chances of a match would be small. Siblings or parents are our best alternative. Do you have any other brothers or sisters?"

"No. I mean, like I told you before, none that I know of.

Both my sister and I were raised by adoptive families. And our biological mother is dead."

"What about your father?"

Andie looked away, embarrassed. She'd anticipated the question, but that didn't make it any easier. "I don't know who that is. I would have to find him."

"How long would that take?"

"How much time do I have?"

Again, the heavy sigh. "Leukemia is curable, but like any cancer, the sooner the better. I wouldn't want to wait more than eight weeks to resume treatment. Ten weeks, tops. And remember, even after a successful transplant, the engraftment process takes anywhere from ten to twenty-eight days. So you have just a few weeks to find him and get him in here for the harvest."

Andie had no reason for optimism, and it made her skin crawl just to think about the perverse terms that inmate Wicassa had spelled out for information about her biological father. But with her sister's life hanging in the balance, only one response came to mind.

"Don't worry. I'll find him. Whatever it takes, I'll find him."

ANDIE LAY AWAKE IN HER BED. Jack was sleeping soundly. The dream that had plagued her for a thousand nights did not return, but only because Andie couldn't fall back to sleep. Her mind's eye could see where her fears were leading her, and she didn't want to go there. The little voice inside her head, however, didn't seem to care what she wanted.

She got up, went to her computer, and pulled up the online newspaper from Seattle. She hadn't told Jack about it. In fact, she had yet to process the newspaper report herself. The very thought of it raised the painful questions all over again, the ones that had caused her so many sleepless nights. The toughest one of all still burned in her mind: When two sisters loved each other the way only sisters can, was there anything one wouldn't do to protect the other? For Andie, the answer, ultimately, had forced her to leave Seattle.

Andie glanced at her cell phone, thinking. She wondered if anyone could understand the choice she had made. She picked up the telephone and went into the bathroom so as not to wake Jack. It was midnight in Seattle. Her brother-in-law answered.

"Steve, hi. It's Andie."

He had not yet gone to bed. "Hey, how are you?"

"Good, thanks. I'm pretty good."

"You sure? It's three a.m. where you are."

"I'm fine, really, I've just . . . I've been awake, thinking. There's something I've been meaning to tell you."

He paused, as if the slight quake in her voice made him wary. "Is something wrong?"

Andie swallowed the lump in her throat. She wasn't sure where to begin, so she skipped to the bottom line. "I'm sorry," she said, her voice just above a whisper.

"Sorry for what?"

"I'm sorry that . . . I couldn't do more for Susan."

"I think we all feel that way, Andie. The truth is, we did everything we could. It just wasn't enough."

She could have argued the point. Steve had been the last one to give up hope, thinking somehow a donor would come through. Andie could have told him about that devil of a man imprisoned in Walla Walla, how he could have led Andie to her biological father and a possible bone marrow transplant that might have saved her sister's life. She could have told him exactly what she didn't do, but she was speechless. No one could fault her for the choice she'd made, no one but herself. Because she knew in her heart that, had she been the one lying on that hospital bed losing the race against time, things would have turned out differently. She would have done it to save her own life. Between sisters, between her and Susan, that was the test. She tried not to dwell on whether Susan would have done it to save Andie's life. (More to the point, would Susan have done it to save Andie's life?)

Finding the words, however, was an impossible feat. She'd never told anyone her secret, and she never would. Period. "Thanks, Steve. That's all I wanted to say. How are you doing?"

"Okay. Hard to believe she's been gone so long. I still have my ups and downs, you know. Just take one day at a time."

"Yeah, I think that's all we can do. You take care, all right?"

"I will. Thanks for calling."

"Good-bye," she said, but her voice was barely audible. As she hung up the phone, she could feel her eyes welling, but she quickly pulled herself together. She was in Miami now. The past was behind her.

She glanced again at the newspaper headline on her computer's LCD: *Three- Strikes Lifer is Paroled.*

It didn't seem possible—three strikes and you're out, no parole. That was the law. But as she read the article for the tenth time in the last two days, the reality sank in:

"An appeals court overturned Mr. Wicassa's armed robbery

conviction—strike number three in his three-strike sentence—making him eligible for immediate release."

Andie turned away from the computer, stunned. Slowly she rose and crossed the bedroom to the nightstand. She slid open the drawer, gripped her pistol, and laid it on the dresser beside her purse. Then she went to the closet and pulled a suitcase down from the shelf.

"What are you doing?" asked Jack.

He was only half-awake, still on his side of the bed, propped up on one elbow.

"I have to go to the airport," she said. "Something's come up."

"What?"

She thought about the carpet of fallen leaves outside her window. "Foliage weekend."

"Foliage?" he said. "It's January."

"Yes," she said, glancing one last time at the online story glowing back at her from the LCD. "And it's definitely peak."

FBI Agent Andie Henning debuted in *Under Cover of Darkness* (2000) and frequently reappears in Grippando's popular series featuring Miami criminal defense lawyer Jack Swyteck.

DEATH, CHEATED

A JACK SWYTECK
SHORT STORY

BY JAMES GRIPPANDO

"The doctor told me I have two years to live," she said. "Three, tops."

My mouth fell open, but words came slowly.

"Damn, Jessie. I'm so sorry."

It wasn't the kind of news you expected to hear from a woman who had only recently celebrated her thirtieth birthday.

It had been six years since I'd last laid eyes on Jessie Merrill. The split had been awkward. Five months after dumping me, Jessie had called for lunch with the hope of giving it another try. By then I was well on my way toward falling hopelessly in love with Cindy Paige, now Mrs. Jack Swyteck—something I never called her unless I wanted to be introduced at cocktail parties as Mr. Cindy Paige. Cindy was more beautiful today than she was then, and I had to admit the same was true of Jessie. That, of course, was no reason to become her lawyer. But it was no reason to turn her away, either. This had nothing to do with the fact that her long auburn hair had once splayed across my pillow. She'd come to me as an old friend in a genuine crisis—and at the moment, she seemed to be on the verge of tears.

I rifled through my desk drawer in search of a tissue. She dug one from her purse.

"It's so hard for me to talk about this," she said.

"I understand."

"I was so damn unprepared for that kind of news."

"Who wouldn't be?"

"I take care of myself. I always have."

"It shows." It wasn't intended as a come-on, just a statement of fact that underscored what a waste this was.

"My first thought was *You're crazy, Doc. This can't be.*"

"Of course."

"I mean, I've never faced anything that I couldn't beat. Then suddenly I'm in the office of some doctor who's basically telling me, 'That's it, game over.' No one bothered to tell me the game had even started."

I could hear the anger in her voice. "I'd be mad, too."

"I was furious. And scared. Especially when he told me what I had."

I didn't ask. I figured she'd tell me, if she wanted me to know.

"He said I had ALS – amyotrophic lateral sclerosis."

"I'm not familiar with that one."

"You probably know it as Lou Gehrig's disease."

"Oh." It was a more ominous-sounding "oh" than intended. She immediately picked up on it.

"So, you know what a horrible illness it is."

"Just from what I heard happened to Lou Gehrig."

"Imagine how it feels to hear that it's going to happen to you. Your mind stays healthy, but your nervous system slowly dies, causing you to lose control of your own body. Eventually your throat muscles fail, you can't swallow anymore, and you either suffocate or choke to death on your own tongue."

She was looking straight at me, and I was the one to blink.

"It's always fatal," she added. "Usually in two to five years."

I wasn't sure what to say. The silence was getting uncomfortable. "I don't know how I can help, but if there's anything I can do, just name it."

"There is."

"Please don't be afraid to ask."

"I'm being sued."

"For what?"

"A million and a half dollars."

I did a double take. "That's a lot of money."

"It's all the money I have in the world."

"Funny," I said. "There was a time when you and I would have thought that *was* all the money in the world."

Her smile was more sad than wistful. "Things change."

"They sure do."

A silence fell between us, an unscripted moment to reminisce.

"Anyway, here's my problem. My *legal* problem. I tried to be responsible about my illness. The first thing I did was get my finances in order. Treatment's expensive, and I wanted to do something extravagant for myself in the time I had left. Maybe a trip to Europe, whatever. I didn't have a lot of money, but I did have a three-million-dollar life insurance policy."

"Why so much?"

"When the stock market tanked a couple years ago, a financial planner talked me into believing that whole-life insurance was a good retirement vehicle. Maybe it would have been worth something by the time I reached sixty-five. But at my age, the cash surrender value is practically zilch. Obviously the death benefit wouldn't kick in until I was dead, which didn't do *me* any good. I wanted a pot of money while I was alive and well enough to enjoy myself."

I nodded, seeing where this was headed. "You did a viatical settlement?"

"You've heard of them?"

"I had a friend with AIDS who did one before he died."

"That's how they got popular, back in the eighties. But the concept works with any terminal disease."

"Is it a done deal?"

"Yes. It sounded like a win-win situation. I sell my three-million-dollar policy to a group of investors for a million and a half dollars. I get a big check right now, when I can use it. They get the three-million-dollar death benefit when I die. They'd basically double their money in two or three years."

"It's a little ghoulish, but I can see the good in it."

"Absolutely. Everybody was satisfied." The sorrow seemed to drain from her expression as she looked at me and said, "Until my symptoms started to disappear."

"Disappear?"

"Yeah. I started getting better."

"But there's no cure for ALS."

"The doctor ran more tests."

I saw a glimmer in her eye. My heart beat faster. "And?"

"They finally figured out I had lead poisoning. It can mimic the symptoms of ALS, but it wasn't nearly enough to kill me."

"You don't have Lou Gehrig's disease?" I said, hopeful.

"No."

"You're not going to die?"

"I'm completely recovered."

A sense of joy washed over me, though I did feel a little manipulated. "Thank God. But why didn't you tell me from the get-go?"

She smiled wryly, then turned serious. "I thought you should know how I felt, even if it was just for a few minutes. This sense of being on the fast track to such an awful death."

"It worked."

"Good. Because I have quite a battle on my hands, legally speaking."

"You want to sue the quack who got the diagnosis wrong?"

"Like I said, at the moment I'm the one being sued over this."

"The viatical investors?" I said.

"You got it. They thought they were coming into three million in at most five years. Turns out they may have to wait another forty or fifty years for their investment to 'mature,' so to speak. They want their million and a half bucks back."

"Them's the breaks."

She smiled. "So you'll take the case?"

I was suddenly thinking about Cindy. Wives and old girlfriends didn't always mix. "I'll need to think about that," I said.

"Don't think too long," she said. "I fired my old lawyer yesterday."

"When does the trial start?"

"Two days ago. Tomorrow's the final day."

"You fired your lawyer in the middle of trial?"

It seemed almost corny, but I could have sworn that she'd batted her eyes. "All's well that ends well, right, Jack? Are you on board or not?"

THE TRIAL WAS IN COURTROOM NINE of the Miami-Dade courthouse, and for the life of me, I couldn't understand why Jessie had been unhappy with her first lawyer. The case was shaping up as a slam-bang winner, the judge had been spitting venom at opposing counsel the entire trial, and the client was a gorgeous redhead who'd once ripped my heart right out of my chest and stomped that sucker flat.

Well, two out of three wasn't bad.

"All rise!"

The lunch break was over, and the lawyers and litigants rose as Judge Antonio Garda Garcia approached the bench. The judge glanced in our direction, as if he couldn't help gathering another eyeful of my client. No surprise there. Jessie wasn't stunningly beautiful, but she was damn close. She carried herself with a confidence that bespoke intelligence, tempered by intermittent moments of apparent vulnerability that made her simply irresistible to the knuckle-dragging, testosterone-toting half of the population. Judge Garcia was as susceptible as the next guy. Beneath that flowing black robe was, after all, a mere mortal—a man. That aside, Jessie was a victim in this case, and it was impossible not to feel sorry for her.

"Good afternoon," said the judge.

"Good afternoon," the lawyers replied, though the judge's

nose was buried in paperwork. Rather than immediately call in the jury, it was Judge Garcia's custom to mount the bench and then take a few minutes to read his mail or finish the crossword puzzle—his way of announcing to all who entered his courtroom that he alone had that rare and special power to silence attorneys and make them sit and wait. Judicial power plays of all sorts seemed to be on the rise in Miami courtrooms, ever since hometown hero Marilyn Melian gave up her day job to star on *The People's Court.* Not every South Florida judge wanted to trace her steps to television stardom, but at least one wannabe in criminal court had taken to encouraging plea bargains by asking, "Deal or no deal?"

I glanced to my left and noticed my client's hand shaking. It stopped the moment she caught me looking. Typical Jessie, never wanting anyone to know she was nervous.

"We're almost home," I whispered. She gave me a tight smile. I knew that smile—before I was married. I fought the impulse to let my mind go there.

The crack of the gavel stirred me from my thoughts. The jury had returned. Judge Garcia had finished perusing his mail, the sports section, or whatever else had caught his attention. Court was back in session.

"Mr. Swyteck, any questions for Dr. Herna?"

I glanced toward the witness stand. Dr. Herna was the physician who'd reviewed Jessie's medical history on behalf of the viatical investors and confirmed the original diagnosis, giving them the green light to invest. He and the investors' lawyer had spent the entire morning trying to convince the jury that, because Jessie didn't actually have ALS, the viatical settlement should be invalidated on the basis of a "mutual mistake." It was my job to prove it was their mistake, nothing mutual about it, too bad, so sad.

I could hardly wait. "Yes, Your Honor," I said, as I approached the witness with a thin, confident smile. "I promise this won't take long."

The courtroom was silent. It was the pivotal moment in the trial, my cross-examination of the plaintiff's star witness. The jury looked on attentively—whites, blacks, Hispanics, a cross-section of Miami. Anyone who wondered if an ethnically diverse community could possibly work together should serve on a jury. The case of *Viatical Solutions, Inc. v. Jessie Merrill* was like dozens of other trials under way in Miami at that very moment—no media, no protestors, no circus ringmaster. It was reassuring to know that the administration of justice in Florida wasn't always the joke people saw on television.

Reassuring for me, anyway. Staring out from the witness stand, Dr. Felix Herna looked anything but calm. My opposing counsel seemed to sense the doctor's anxiety. Parker Aimes was a savvy-enough plaintiffs' attorney to sprint to his feet and do something about it.

"Judge, could we have a five-minute break, please?"

"We just got back from lunch," he said, snarling.

"I know but—"

"But nothing," the judge said, peering out over the top of his wire-rimmed reading glasses, "Counselor, I just checked my horoscope, and it says there's loads of leisure time in my near future. So, Mr. Swyteck, if you please."

With the judge talking astrology, I was beginning to rethink my restored faith in the justice system. "Thank you, Your Honor."

All eyes of the jurors followed as I approached the witness, I planted myself firmly, using height and body language to convey a trial lawyer's greatest tool: control.

"Dr. Herna, you'll agree with me that ALS is a serious disease, won't you?"

He shifted nervously, as if distrustful of even the most innocuous question, "Of course."

"It attacks the nervous system, breaks down the tissues, kills the motor neurons?"

"That's correct."

"Victims eventually lose the ability to control their legs?"

"Yes."

"Their hands and arms as well?"

"Yes."

"Their abdominal muscles?"

"That's correct, yes. It destroys the neurons that control the body's voluntary muscles. Muscles controlled by conscious thought."

"Speech becomes unclear? Hearing and swallowing become difficult?"

"Yes."

"Breathing may become impossible?"

"It does affect the tongue and pharyngeal muscles. Eventually, all victims must choose between prolonging their life on a ventilator or asphyxiation."

"Suffocation," I said. "Not a very pleasant way to die."

"Death is rarely pleasant, Mr. Swyteck."

"Unless you're a viatical investor."

A juror nodded with agreement.

"Objection."

"Uh," said the judge, "sustained."

I moved on, knowing I'd tweaked the opposition, "Is it fair to say that once ALS starts, there's no way to stop it?"

"Miracles may happen, but the basic assumption in the medical community is that the disease is fatal, its progression relentless. Fifty percent of people die within two years, eighty percent within five."

"Sounds like an ideal scenario for a viatical settlement," I said.

"Objection."

"I'll rephrase it. True or false, Doctor: The basic assumption of viatical investors is that the patient will die soon."

He looked at me as if the question were ridiculous. "Of course that's true. That's how they make their money."

"You'd agree, then, that a proper diagnosis is a key component of the investment decision?"

"True again."

"That's why the investors hired you, isn't it? They relied on *you* to confirm that Ms. Merrill had ALS."

"They hired me to review her doctor's diagnosis."

"How many times did you physically examine her?"

"None."

"How many times did you meet with her?"

"None."

"How many times did you speak with her?"

"None," he said, his tone defensive. "You're making this sound worse than it really was. The reviewing physician in a viatical settlement rarely if ever examines the patient. It was my job to review Ms. Merrill's medical history as presented to me by her treating physician. I then made a determination as to whether the diagnosis was based on sound medical judgment."

"So you were fully aware that Dr. Marsh's diagnosis was 'clinically possible ALS.'"

"Yes."

"*Possible* ALS," I repeated, making sure the judge and jury caught it. "Which means that it could possibly be something else."

"Her symptoms, though minor, were entirely consistent with the early stages of the disease."

"But the very diagnosis—possible ALS—made it clear that it could be something other than ALS. And you knew that."

The doctor was wringing his hands. "You have to understand that there's no magic bullet, no single test to determine whether a patient has ALS. The diagnosis is in many ways a process of elimination. A series of tests are run over a period of months to rule out other possible illnesses. In the early stages, a seemingly healthy woman like Jessie Merrill could have ALS and have no idea that anything's seriously wrong with her body, apart from the fact that maybe her foot falls asleep, or she fumbles with her car keys, or is having difficulty swallowing."

"You're not suggesting that your investors plunked down a million and a half dollars based solely on the fact that Ms. Merrill was dropping her car keys."

"No."

"In fact, your investors rejected the investment proposal at first, didn't they?"

"An investment based on a diagnosis of clinically possible ALS was deemed too risky."

"They decided to invest only after you spoke with Dr. Marsh, correct?"

"I did speak with him."

I gestured toward the jury, as if inviting them into the conversation. "Would you share with the jury Dr. Marsh's exact words, please?"

Even the judge looked up, his interest sufficiently piqued. Dr. Herna shifted his weight again, obviously reluctant.

"Let me say at the outset that Dr. Marsh is one of the most respected neurologists in Florida. I knew that his diagnosis of clinically possible ALS was based upon strict adherence to the diagnostic criteria established by the World Federation of Neurology. But I also knew that he was an experienced physician who had seen more cases of ALS than just about any other doctor in Miami. So I asked him to put the strict criteria aside. I asked him to talk to me straight but off the record: Did he think Jessie Merrill had ALS?"

"I'll ask the question again: What did Dr. Marsh tell you?"

Herna looked at his lawyer, then at me, and said, "He told me that if he were a betting man, he'd bet on ALS."

"As it turns out, Ms. Merrill didn't have ALS, did she?"

"Obviously not. Dr. Marsh was dead wrong."

"Excuse me, Doctor. He wasn't wrong. Dr. Marsh's diagnosis was clinically *possible* ALS. You knew that he was still monitoring the patient, still conducting tests."

"I also know what he told me. He told me to bet on ALS."

"Only after you pushed him to speculate prematurely."

"As a colleague with the utmost respect for the man, I asked for his honest opinion."

"You urged him to *guess*. You pushed for an answer because Ms. Merrill was a tempting investment opportunity."

"That's not true."

"You were afraid that if you waited for a conclusive diagnosis, she'd be snatched up by another group of viatical investors."

"All I know is that Dr. Marsh said he'd bet on ALS. That was good enough for me."

I moved closer, tightening the figurative grip, "It wasn't Ms. Merrill who made the wrong diagnosis, was it?"

"No."

"As far as she knew, a horrible death was just two or three years away."

"I don't know what she was thinking."

"Yes, you do," I said sharply. "When you reviewed her medical file and coughed up a million and a half dollars to buy her life insurance policy, you became her second opinion. You convinced her that she was going to die."

He fell stone silent, as if suddenly he realized the grief he'd caused her—as if finally he understood my animosity.

I continued: "Ms. Merrill never told you she had a confirmed case of ALS, did she?"

"No."

"She never guaranteed you that she'd die in two years."

"No."

"All she did was give you her medical records."

"That's all I saw."

"And you made a professional judgment as to whether she was going to live or die."

"I did."

"And you bet on death."

"In a manner of speaking."

"You bet on ALS."

"Yes."

"And you lost."

He didn't answer. I couldn't let go.

"Doctor, you and your investors rolled the dice and lost. Isn't that what really happened here?"

He hesitated, then answered: "It didn't turn out the way we thought it would."

"Great reason to file a lawsuit."

"Objection."

"Sustained."

I didn't push it, but a little sarcasm had telegraphed to the jury the question I most wanted answered: *Don't you think this woman has been through enough without you suing her, jerk?*

"Are you finished, Mr. Swyteck?" asked Judge Garcia.

"Yes. I think that wraps things up."

I turned away from the witness and headed back to my chair. I could see the gratitude in Jessie's eyes, but far more palpable was the dagger in my back that was Dr. Herna's angry glare.

Jessie leaned closer and whispered, "Nice work."

"Yeah," I said, fixing on the word she'd chosen. "I was entirely too *nice*."

JESSIE AND I WERE SEATED on the courthouse steps, casting cookie crumbs to pigeons as we awaited notification that the jury had reached a verdict.

"What do you think they'll do?" she asked.

I paused. The tiers of granite outside the Miami-Dade courthouse were the judicial equivalent of the Oracle of Delphi, where lawyers were called upon daily to hazard a wild-ass guess about a process that was ultimately unpredictable. I would have liked to tell her there was nothing to worry about, that in twenty minutes we'd be cruising toward Miami Beach, the top down on my beloved Mustang convertible, the CD player totally cranked with an obnoxiously loud version of the old hit song from the rock band Queen "We Are the Champions."

But my career had brought too many surprises to be that unequivocal.

"I have a good feeling," I said. "But with a jury, you never know."

I savored the last bit of cream from the better half of an Oreo, then tossed the rest of the cookie to the steps below. A chorus of gray wings fluttered as hungry pigeons scurried after the treat. In seconds it was in a hundred pieces. The victors flew off into the warm, crystal-blue skies that marked February in Miami.

Jessie said, "Either way, I guess this is it."

"We might have an appeal if we lose."

"I was speaking more on a personal level." She laid her hand on my forearm and said, "You did a really great thing for me, stepping in and taking my case in midstream. But in a few minutes it will all be over. And then I guess I'll never see you again."

"That's actually a good thing. In my experience, reuniting with an old client usually means they've been sued or indicted all over again."

"I've had my fill of that, thank you."

"I know you have."

I glanced toward the hot-dog vendor on the crowded sidewalk along Flagler Street, then back at Jessie. She hadn't shifted her gaze away from me, and her hand was still resting on my forearm. A little too touchy-feely today. I rose and buried my hands in my pants pockets.

"Jack, there's something I want to tell you."

The conversation seemed to be drifting beyond the attorney-client relationship, and I didn't want to go there. I was her lawyer, nothing more, never mind the past.

"Before you say anything," I said, "there's something I should tell you."

"Really?" she said.

I sat on the step beside her. "I noticed that Dr. Marsh was back in the courtroom today. He's obviously concerned."

My abrupt return to law talk seemed to confuse her.

"Concerned about me, you mean?" she said.

"I'd say his exact concern is whether you plan to sue him. We haven't talked much about this, but you probably do have a case against him."

"Sue him? For what?"

"Malpractice, of course. He eventually got your diagnosis right, but not until you went through severe emotional distress. He should have targeted lead poisoning as the cause of your neurological problems much earlier than he did. Especially after you told him about the renovations to your condo. The dust that comes with sanding off old lead-based paint in houses built before nineteen seventy-eight is a pretty common source of lead poisoning,"

"But he's the top expert in Miami."

"He's still capable of being wrong. He is human, after all."

She looked off to the middle distance. "That's the perfect word for him. He was *so* human. He took such special care of me."

"How do you mean?"

"Some doctors are ice cold, no bedside manner at all. Dr. Marsh was very sympathetic, very compassionate. It's not that common for someone under the age of forty to get ALS, and he took a genuine interest in me."

"In what way?"

"Not in the way you're thinking," she said, giving me a playful kick in the shin.

"I'm not thinking anything," I said, lying.

"I'll give you a perfect example. One of the most important tests I had was the EMG. That's the one where they hook you up to the electrodes to see if there's any nerve damage."

"I know. I saw the report."

"Yeah, but *all* you saw was the report. The actual test can be pretty scary, especially when you're worried that you might have something as awful as Lou Gehrig's disease. Most neurologists have a technician do the test. But Dr. Marsh knew how freaked out I was about this. I didn't want some technician to conduct the test, and then I'd have to wait another week for the doctor to interpret the results, and then wait another two weeks for a follow-up appointment where the results would finally be explained to me. So he ran the test himself, immediately. There aren't a lot of doctors who would do that for their patients in this world of mismanaged care."

"You're right about that."

"I could give you a dozen other examples. He's a great doctor and a real gentleman. I don't need to sue Dr. Marsh. The investors can have my three million dollars in life insurance when I die. As far as I'm concerned, a million and a half dollars is plenty for me."

I couldn't disagree. It was one more pleasant reminder that she was no longer the self-centered twenty-something-year-old of another decade. And neither was I.

"You're making the right decision," I said.

"I've made a few good ones in my lifetime," she said, her smile fading.

"And a few bad ones, too."

I was at a loss for the right response, and preferred to let it go. But she followed up.

"Have you ever wondered what would have happened if we hadn't broken up?"

"No."

"Liar."

"Let's not talk about that," I said.

"Why not? Isn't that just a teensy-weensy part of the reason you jumped into my case?"

"No."

"Liar."

"Stop calling me a liar," I said.

"Stop lying."

"What do you want me to say?"

She moved closer, invading my space again. "Just answer one question for me," she said.

"I want you to be completely honest. And if you are, I'll totally drop this, okay?" "All right. One."

"If I had hired you from the beginning of this case—if you and I had been lawyer and client for six months instead of just a couple days—do you think something would have happened between us?"

"No."

"Why not?"

"That's two questions," I said.

"Why do you think nothing would have happened?"

"Because I'm married."

She flashed a thin smile, nodding knowingly. "Interesting answer."

"What's so interesting about it? That's the answer."

"Yes, but you could have said something a little different, like: 'Because I love my wife.' Instead, you said, 'Because I'm married.'"

"It comes down to the same thing."

"No. One comes from the heart. The other is just a matter of playing by the rules."

I didn't answer. Jessie had always been a smart girl, but that was perhaps the most perceptive thing I'd ever heard her say. The digital pager vibrated on my belt. I checked it eagerly, then looked at Jessie and said, "Jury's back."

She didn't move, still waiting for me to respond in some way to her words. I just gathered myself up and said, "Can't keep the judge and jury waiting."

Without more, she rose and followed me up the courthouse steps.

IN MINUTES WE WERE BACK IN COURTROOM nine, and I could feel the butterflies swirling in my belly. This wasn't the most legally complicated case I'd ever handled, but I wanted to win it for Jessie. It had nothing to do with the fact that my client was a woman who'd once rejected me and that this was my chance to prove what a great lawyer I was. Jessie deserved to win. Period. It was that simple.

Right. Was anything ever that simple?

My client and I stood impassively at our place behind the mahogany table for the defense. Plaintiff's counsel stood alone on the other side of the courtroom, at the table closest to the jury box. His client, a corporation, hadn't bothered to send a representative for the rendering of the verdict. Perhaps they'd expected the worst, a prospect that seemed to have stimulated some public interest. A reporter from the local paper was seated in the first row, and behind her in the public gallery were other folks I didn't recognize. One face, however, was entirely familiar: Dr. Joseph Marsh, Jessie's neurologist, was standing in the rear of the courtroom.

A paddle fan wobbled overhead as the decision makers returned to the jury box in single file. Each of them looked straight ahead, sharing not a glance with either the plaintiff or the defendant. Professional jury consultants could have argued for days as to the significance of their body language—whether it was good or bad if they made eye contact with the plaintiff, the defendant, the lawyers, the judge, or no one at all. To me, it was all pop psychology, unreliable even when the foreman winked at your client and mouthed the words, *It's in the bag, baby.*

"Has the jury reached a verdict?" asked the judge.

"We have," announced the forewoman. The all-important slip of paper went from the jury box, to the bailiff, and finally to the judge. He inspected it for less than half a second, showing no reaction. "Please announce the verdict."

I felt my client's manicured fingernails digging into my biceps.

"In the case of *Viatical Solutions, Inc. v. Jessie Merrill*, we the jury find in favor of the defendant."

I suddenly found myself locked in what felt like a full-body embrace, Jessie trembling in my arms. Had I not been there to hold her, she would have fallen to the floor. A tear trickled down her cheek as she looked me in the eye and whispered, "Thank you."

"You're so welcome."

I released her, but she held me a moment longer—a little too long and too publicly, perhaps, to suit a married man. Then again, plenty of overjoyed clients had hugged me in the past, even big burly men who were homophobic to the core. Like them, Jessie had simply gotten carried away with the moment.

Right?

"Your Honor, we have a motion," said the lawyer for Viatical Solutions, Inc., as he approached the lectern. He seemed on the verge of an explosion, which was understandable. One and a half million dollars had just slipped through his fingers. Six months ago he'd written an arrogant letter to Jessie telling her that her viatical settlement wasn't worth the paper it was written on. Now Jessie was cool, and he was the fool.

God, I loved winning.

"What's your motion?" the judge asked.

Parker Aimes cleared his throat. "We ask that the court enter judgment for the plaintiff notwithstanding the verdict. The evidence does not support—"

"Save it," said the judge.

"Excuse me?"

"You heard me, Mr. Aimes." With that, Judge Garcia unleashed a veritable tongue-lashing. He truly seemed taken with Jessie. At least a half-dozen times in the span of two minutes he derided the suit against her as "frivolous and mean-spirited." He not only denied the plaintiff's post-trial motion, but he so completely clobbered them that I was beginning to wish I had invited Cindy downtown to watch.

On second thought, it was just as well that she'd missed that big hug Jessie had given me in her excitement over the verdict.

The judge leaned forward and used the friendly tone he reserved only for non-lawyers. "Ladies and gentlemen of the jury, thank you for your service. We are adjourned."

With a bang of the judge's gavel, it was all over.

Jessie was a millionaire.

"Time to celebrate," she said.

"You go right ahead. You've earned it."

"You're coming, too, buster. Drinks are on me."

I checked my watch. "All right. It's early for me, but maybe a beer."

"One beer? Wimp."

"Lush."

"Lawyer."

"Now you're hitting way below the belt."

We shared a smile, then headed for the exit. The courtroom had already cleared, but a small crowd was gathering at the elevator. Most had emerged from another courtroom, but I recognized a few spectators from Jessie's trial.

Among them was Dr. Marsh.

The elevator doors opened, but I tugged at Jessie's elbow. "Let's wait for the next one," I told her.

"There's room," said Jessie. A dozen people packed into the crowded car. In all the jostling for position, a janitor and his bucket came between Jessie and me. The doors closed, and as if it were an immutable precept of universal elevator etiquette, all conversation ceased. The lighted numbers overhead marked our silent descent. The doors opened two floors down. Three passengers got out, four more got in. I kept my eyes forward but noticed that, in the shuffle, Dr. Marsh had wended his way from the back of the car to a spot directly beside Jessie.

The elevator stopped again. Another exchange of passengers, two exiting, two more getting in. I kept my place in front, near the control panel. As the doors closed, Jessie moved all the way to the far corner. Dr. Marsh managed to find an opening right beside her.

Was he actually pursuing her?

It was too crowded for me to turn around completely, but I could see Jessie and her former physician in the convex mirror in the opposite corner of the elevator. Discreetly, I kept an eye on both of them. Marsh had blown the diagnosis of ALS, but he was a smart guy. Surely he'd anticipated that Jessie would speak to her lawyer about suing him for malpractice. If it was his intention to corner Jessie in the elevator and breathe a few threatening words into her ear, I would be all over him.

No more stops. The elevator was on the express route to the lobby. I glanced at the lighted numbers above the door, then back at the mirror.

My heart nearly stopped; I couldn't believe my eyes.

It had lasted only a split second, but what I'd seen was unmistakable. Obviously, Jessie and the doctor hadn't noticed the mirror, hadn't realized that I was watching them even though they were standing behind me.

They'd locked fingers, as if holding hands, then released.

For one chilling moment, I couldn't breathe.

The elevator doors opened. I held the Door Open button to allow the others to exit. Dr. Marsh passed without a word, without so much as looking at me. Jessie emerged last. I took her by the arm and pulled her into an alcove near the bank of pay telephones.

"What the hell did you just do in there?"

She shook free of my grip. "Nothing."

"I was watching in the mirror. I saw you and Marsh hold hands."

"Are you crazy?"

"Apparently. Crazy to have trusted you."

She shook her head, scoffing. "You're a real piece of work, you know that, Swyteck? That's what I couldn't stand when we were dating, you and your stupid jealousy."

"This has nothing to do with jealousy. You just held hands with the doctor who supposedly started this whole problem by misdiagnosing you with ALS. You owe me a damn good explanation, lady."

"We don't owe you anything."

It struck me cold, the way she'd said *we*. I was suddenly thinking of our conversation on the courthouse steps just minutes earlier, where Jessie had heaped such praise on the kind and considerate doctor.

"Now I see why Dr. Marsh performed the diagnostic tests himself," I said. "It had nothing to do with his compassion. You never had any symptoms of ALS. You never even had lead poisoning. The tests were fakes, weren't they?"

She just glared and said, "It's like I told you: we don't owe you anything."

"What do you expect me to do? Ignore what I just saw?"

"Yes. Like my first lawyer. The one I fired before I hired you. He just keeps his mouth shut. And you will, too. If you're smart."

"Is that some kind of threat?"

"Do yourself a favor, okay? Forget you ever knew me. Move on with your life."

Those were the exact words she'd used to dump me years earlier.

She started away, and then stopped, as if unable to resist one more shot.

"I feel sorry for you, Swyteck. I feel sorry for anyone who goes through life just playing by the rules."

As she turned and disappeared into the crowded lobby, I felt a gaping pit in the bottom of my stomach. Ten years a trial lawyer. I'd represented thieves, swindlers, even cold-blooded murderers. I'd never claimed to be the world's smartest man, but never before had I even come close to letting this happen. The realization was sickening.

Jessie had cheated death.

Her investors.

And me.

SAMMY AND ME

A TRIBUTE TO MY FOUR-LEGGED FRIEND

JAMES GRIPPANDO

I write outdoors. Writing in my own backyard connects me to the Florida setting that figures so prominently in all ten of my novels. My outdoor office has these essentials: a patio table and chair, a big shade umbrella, a laptop computer, a hammock, a hot tub, and a swimming pool. The cell phone is optional.

For nine years, my office mate and principal workday diversion was my Golden Retriever. Sam lay at my feet as I wrote, and every time I stood up for a break, he would dash toward the swimming pool. He loved the pool, which is somewhat ironic. He was born in a puppy mill and never saw a blade of grass until we took him home at twelve weeks. At the time, I wasn't even looking for a pet, and it was actually my best friend who bought him. After just twenty-four hours, my friend decided that he couldn't handle a dog and wanted to return him. "He's not a shirt," I told him. "You can't just take him back." The truth was, I was already in love with Sam, and I couldn't stand the thought of him going back to that mill. So my wife and I adopted him, even though Tiffany was in her eighth month, pregnant with our first child. Sam would be there for the birth of all three of our children. He was in some ways our "first," but more like our "fourth," loyally and dutifully taking his place a notch lower on the totem pole with each new addition to the family. He never seemed to mind when the kids tugged at his ears and tail or climbed up on his back. In fact, I'd say he *loved* it.

Sam was always good for a diversion, or a laugh. He was so crazy as a puppy that my daughter renamed him "Sammy Cu-koo." He didn't discover his bark until he was almost two years old, and that strange sound coming from his own mouth nearly scared him half to death. He brought the newspaper to my "office" every morning, and then, without fail, he would head for the pool. He'd get his toy, drop it at my feet, and lay there until I was ready to break away from my computer and play with him. My job was to toss his toy into the pool. He would wait for it to sink all the way to the bottom. As soon as I said "Get it, Sam," he'd dive in headfirst and bring it up from the depths. It was our little "stupid pet trick," which he never got tired of.

Sam and I did eleven novels in nine years together, all in our outdoor office.

In December 2005 life was finally getting back to normal after all the hurricane clean up. Sam, however, seemed anything but normal. We thought he had a cold. By New Year's Day he really wasn't himself, so we took him to the vet. It wasn't a cold or the flu. It was cancer. His liver was shutting down. Our vet ran tests, but the news just kept getting worse. After keeping him overnight, she said it was time to think about putting him to sleep. She assured us that Sam was not in pain, so we brought him home on Friday morning. He actually perked up a little at home, but we knew he was very sick. By Friday night, we were able to interest him in taking water, Gatorade, and chicken soup from a syringe. The soup made his tail wag, our last glimpse of the old Sammy. We feared that on Monday morning we would have to take him back to the vet for the last time.

On Saturday night, Sam wanted to sleep at the far end of the house, where he'd never slept before. We laid him on a blanket, made him comfortable, hugged and kissed him good-night, and went to bed. At 2:00 a.m., I woke suddenly. I went to his spot, but he was gone. I checked around the house but couldn't find him. Finally, I saw. He had forced himself up and hobbled over to the door to our daughter's bedroom. He was in one of his favorite spots, close to the children. It was there that he died.

Later that morning, for the first time in almost ten years, I walked to the end of the driveway and got the Sunday newspaper myself. On the front page of the *Miami Herald* book section was a rave review for *Got the Look*, my new book. Without question, it was the most glowing review I had ever received as an author. My wife read it and wept. "Honey," I said, "it's a great review, but it's just a *review*." She pointed to the byline. "The guy who wrote it," she said. "His name is Sam."

Tiffany is no Shirley MacLaine, but she doesn't believe in meaningless coincidences, either. How could it be that the best review I'd ever received appeared on this morning, of all mornings, and had been written by a reviewer named Sam? I didn't know what to make of it, but I didn't dwell on it. I had to take our Sam's body to the vet for cremation.

When I returned, my son was playing in the yard. He came into the house and asked, "Daddy, what are those balloons doing in our swimming pool?" I had no idea what he was talking about. I went outside. Sure enough, two balloons were floating in our pool, tied together with a long blue ribbon.

I can only surmise that, somewhere around us, there had been a child's birthday party on Saturday afternoon. These helium balloons had broken free, drifted overnight, and finally come to rest on our property. It seems only fitting that they landed in our swimming pool. In Sam's pool. On the day he died.

James Grippando is a New York Times bestselling author. He writes in Coral Gables, Florida, where he lives with his wife, Tiffany, and their three children, Kaylee, Ryan, and Ainsley. They will never forget Sam.

Acknowledgments

Thank you …

To my friend, Tom Bales, whose real-life work on the world's largest telescope has inspired children all over the world.

To Kevin Smith, who tried very hard to help me understand the complexities of time synchronization. Kevin was my go-to guy on so many "techie" issues in past novels. You are missed and remembered fondly, Kevin.

To my beta readers, Janis Koch and Gloria Villa, who are indispensable members of "Team Grippando."

To my friends at Nightstand, Jared and Antoinette, who from the very beginning embraced *The Penny Jumper* and loved it as much as I did.

To my daughter Ainsley, who at age three really did choose "the cornucopia."

And to my wife Tiffany, for loving a dreamer whose head is in the clouds—except on clear nights, when I'm gazing at the stars.